TPS SURPLUS

OPERATION PEEG

OPERATION PEEG

by JONATHAN GATHORNE-HARDY

Illustrated by GLO COALSON

J. B. LIPPINCOTT COMPANY   PHILADELPHIA AND NEW YORK

F
GAT

For Jenny and Benjamin

U.S. Library of Congress Cataloging in Publication Data

Gathorne-Hardy, Jonathan.
  Operation Peeg.

  SUMMARY: Jarred loose by an explosion, an island occupied by a young
girl and her two companions floats out to sea under the command of two
British soldiers who believe that World War II is still in progress.
  [1. Adventure stories] I. Coalson, Glo, illus. II. Title.
PZ7.G2250p3   [Fic]   74-8908
ISBN-0-397-31594-5

4-8

CONTENTS

1

SETTLING IN AT ALDEBURGH

WHEN LORD AND LADY CHARRINGTON arrived back from their visit to America, Lord Charrington decided to change the life of his wife, himself, and his daughter Jane in two major ways.

First, he stopped being a Lord. Lady Charrington was quite interested when he told her, until she discovered this also meant she had to stop being a Lady. Then she was appalled. But Lord Charrington had been deeply impressed by the democratic way of life in America, and nothing his wife could do would shift him. "No, my dear," he said calmly, "from now on we are plain Mr. and Mrs."

The second thing he did was to take them away from the enormous old castle in Cornwall, called Curl Castle, where the Charringtons had lived for three hundred years. "Now we are common or garden Mr. and Mrs.," he said, "we must live like other people. We will rent a little house from some town council or other and give Curl to the nation."

Lady Charrington, or rather Mrs. Charrington, as she

was now called, was still so horrified at not being a Lady that at first she scarcely noticed this second blow, but in fact it proved to be the first difficulty in their new democratic way of life.

Mr. Charrington had chosen No. 2 in a row of thirty-five brand-new empty council houses which had been built at the back of Aldeburgh, where he had decided to live. But when they arrived in their Land Rover, followed by forty large furniture vans· containing very nearly everything from Curl Castle, they realized at once they would need either a great deal less furniture or else something a great deal larger to live in.

Mr. Charrington was a large, decisive man. He liked nothing better than a firm decision. He put Mrs. Charrington, Jane, and the Charringtons' housekeeper, Mrs. Deal, in the Wentworth Hotel, made the furniture vans park outside the Golf Club, and hurried off to find the chairman of the Aldeburgh Rural District Council.

Fortunately, the Housing Committee of the District Council was having a meeting that very morning. Mr. Charrington spoke to them persuasively and decisively for ten minutes, and they soon agreed that, though they could not sell council houses, if he gave them enough money to build two council houses, they would let him rent one council house for 999 years. If he gave them enough to build four council houses, they would rent him two council houses, and so on.

Mr. Charrington returned with beaming face to the Wentworth Hotel.

"My darling," he said to his wife, "I have rented Number One and Number Three for nine hundred and ninety-nine years!"

"Rented? Oh, dear," said Mrs. Charrington, who had been taught that it was always better to buy houses. "Do

8

you think that's wise? What happens when they no longer belong to us? What then?"

"Nine hundred ninety-nine years," said Mr. Charrington a bit impatiently. "Nine hundred ninety-nine years, darling."

"Yes, but you know how time flies," said Mrs. Charrington. "Still, I suppose it's better than nothing."

For the rest of the morning the men worked hard, and by lunchtime Nos. 1, 2, and 3 council houses were full of furniture and only four of the furniture vans were empty. Mr. Charrington hurried back to the Housing Committee and rented Nos. 4 and 5 for 999 years. By the end of the week all the furniture vans were empty, and Mr. Charrington had rented all the council houses for 999 years at a cost of £172,500.

The second difficulty they encountered was about Jane's school. Mr. Charrington had originally decided that she should go to a state school rather than a private one.

"You will agree, my darling," he said, "that in our new position—plain Mr. and Mrs., a single servant, living in a council house—"

"Houses," said Mrs. Charrington.

"Houses—you will agree that Jane should go to the sort of school any other boy or girl in her sort of position goes to."

Mrs. Charrington did not agree. She did not, in fact, think there *was* anyone else in Jane's position. After some discussion, they reached a compromise. Jane was to be sent to a school in the northwest of Scotland, which advertised itself as being ready to take anyone—"of whatever color, creed, or background."

The fees at Peeg School were £1000 a year, and there were, therefore, very few of the sorts of girls Mr. Charrington had meant. And there were other things that might have stopped him sending Jane there had he known of them. The headmistress, Miss Boyle, though very fair and not unkind, was extremely strict. She believed in physical fitness and beating in "extreme cases." Football, hiking, and tossing the caber were all compulsory. About twice a year there would be "an extreme case," and some frightened little girl would have her bottom smacked with Miss Boyle's slipper.

Also, Peeg School was in a very wild and remote place. Peeg House was very large, with pinnacles and pointed windows. It had first been the home of Lord Kinross, Laird of Peeg, and then a hotel. It stood all alone in the middle of a small island called the Isle of Peeg. It was, in fact, not quite an island at all because it was joined to the shore by a narrow strip of land, or causeway.

The Isle of Peeg was a mile long and three-quarters of a mile wide. The school was in the middle, in a small valley. All round it the heather-covered ground rose gently up and stretched away to the low cliffs which faced the sea. Behind the school and toward the front of the island there was quite a steep hill, which rose high enough to be called Mount Peeg, and from its top you could see the whole island and across to the mainland of Scotland. Halfway up the island and two hundred yards out from the shore there was a large rock in the sea called Little Peeg.

The weather on Peeg was extremely wet; everywhere you went you could hear the trickling sound of water and had to be careful to avoid bogs and marshes. Even at the top of Mount Peeg there was a small pool with reeds and moss. In winter there were terrible storms; you could see from the school the plumes of spray where the waves dashed above the cliffs. Even in summer, when the girls would pick the velvet moss bulging up onto the tops of the rocks or scream at the black slugs, there were sudden rainstorms. But for most of the time, winter and summer, it was not so much rain as mist, a perpetual muslin of mist in which you only had to stand for ten minutes to be soaking wet, and which trailed gloomily over the heather or came drifting down into the valley to lie for days in patches and pockets and hang caught in the damp needles of the pine trees growing at the lower end of the burn.

Jane did not really enjoy her first term. She hated the school smells of floor polish and cooking cabbage. She kept very quiet and was careful to be very good. She made one friend—a girl called Jemima Garing. It was not till the third week of her second term that she began to behave more like her real self. And it was in the third week, also, that two things happened, quite independently of Jane's behavior, which were to start what *The Sunday Times* was later to describe as "one of the most extraordinary adventures of our time."

2

THE FIRST EXPLOSION

A FAVORITE GAME for naughty girls at Peeg School was shooting butter pats at the dining room ceiling. You stuck your knife blade into the gap underneath the table top, pulled down the handle with a butter pat balanced on it, and let go. With a faint vibrating *brrrrr* the butter soared into the air and sometimes stuck to the ceiling.

It was this that Jane was trying to do one dreary October day in the third week of the term. Three times the butter sprang into the air, and three times another yellow blob appeared on the ceiling. All round the dining room the girls chattered and talked at high tea, doing their best to eat boiled cabbage. But all the little girls at the same table as Jane giggled nervously and kept looking to see if the prefect was watching. "Do be careful," they whispered, "don't get caught."

Jane smiled. "One more," she said boldly.

As before, the small round pat shot from the knife handle. But this time, instead of rising into the air, it went forward. It skimmed over the head of the prefect, sped like a tiny flying saucer across five tables, and then, before

Jane's horrified eyes, fell out of sight at the far end of the dining room.

For three minutes nothing happened. Jane began to eat her cabbage very fast and interestedly. Then, suddenly, there came the tinkle of the staff bell, which was only rung at the end of tea or for very important announcements. Out of the corner of her eye, Jane saw the thick figure of Miss Boyle standing at the end of the staff table, bell in hand.

"Girls," cried Miss Boyle, "a butter pat has just landed on the table in front of my plate."

There was dead silence. Everyone was far too frightened of Miss Boyle to dare even to smile.

"Who did it?" said Miss Boyle. "I am waiting. Come on. The girl who launched this projectile please stand forward immediately."

Jane stopped breathing. She imagined for a second that she *was* the cabbage, or even a worm inside the cabbage, boiled and dead, quite beyond the reach of headmistresses and slippers. Everyone in the large, dimly lit dining room stared at their plates.

"Unless the culprit stands forth immediately," said Miss Boyle, her bell giving a tiny tinkle of emphasis, "the entire school will be kept in tomorrow. No one will go to the Glenelg Highland Games."

At this dreadful threat, dreadful at least to the Scots girls at Peeg School, a murmur broke out. Jane felt herself turning into one huge blush. Clenching her teeth, she very slowly stood up.

"*I* threw the butter, Miss Boyle."

Like sixty torches, all the heads turned toward her, including Miss Boyle's. "Who's that?" she called.

"It's Jane Charrington, First Form, Miss Boyle," called the prefect officiously.

"I will see Jane Charrington later," said Miss Boyle. "School may resume high tea."

After tea, all the girls disappeared to their various evening duties. The First Form had an hour's free time in their common room and then had to go to bed. The moment they were all together, they crowded round Jane. "It's bound to be an Extreme Case." "The Boil will beat you black and blue." "Poor Jane." They were all very sympathetic.

But after half an hour Miss Boyle had still not called her. Bathtime came; bedtime; it was not until nearly lights-out, when Jane was sitting up in bed in her nightie, that there came the *slap, slap, slap* of slippered feet running down the corridor.

"Jane Charrington to see the Boil!"

It was not, after all, so terrible. The walk along the dark, polish-smelling corridors was terrifying. So was the wait outside Miss Boyle's study. But once inside, Jane suddenly felt quite calm and confident. Miss Boyle stood facing her, legs as usual wide apart. Her heavy, lined face was serious. In her hand she held the large blue *Report Book* in which were entered details of all the school punishments.

"Come in and sit down," she said. "I will be brisk and to the point. I always like to get to the point, and I would like all my girls to do the same. Now—why did you throw the butter?"

"I don't know, Miss Boyle," said Jane.

"You don't know," said Miss Boyle. She walked over to the chair by the fire and pointed to one opposite. When they were both sitting down she took off her spectacles and leaned forward. "I see from the *Report Book* that this is the first time you have seriously misbehaved. Now, at one jump, you become an Extreme Case. Because, make no mistake," said Miss Boyle, "this is an Extreme Case. Do you know why?"

Jane wondered whether to say yes or no. She decided the best thing to do was to mumble. "Mmmmm," she said.

"An ambiguous answer, Jane," said Miss Boyle, "that is to say, an answer which could mean two things—yes or no. I shall explain why throwing butter is an Extreme Case."

Then Miss Boyle began one of her famous talkings-to. She spoke in her firm voice for thirty-five minutes. Quite soon Jane stopped listening and began planning. She was quite sure this was not the sort of school her mother and father meant her to go to. It was difficult to describe it to them in a letter, so the best thing would be to run away to Aldeburgh and tell them. She would do this tomorrow. Once or twice Miss Boyle interrupted Jane's thoughts by asking questions.

"What do you suppose would happen if everyone in the dining room threw butter?" she said at one moment.

Caught off guard, Jane began, "Why, I think it would . . ." But suddenly noticing the stout leather slippers, which in the evenings replaced her brogues, sticking out below Miss Boyle's long tweed skirt, she ended humbly, ". . . it would be terrible."

"Terrible," agreed Miss Boyle, imagining it.

In the end, however, she grew quite kind. "It was brave of you to stand up in the dining room," she said. "You have an excellent record. You come of rich and distinguished parents. In fact, *very* rich and *very* distinguished. Yes. In the circumstances, although an Extreme Case, I have decided not to exact the usual penalty. Instead, out of the whole school, you alone will miss the Glenelg Highland Games. You will stay here and write out two thousand times 'I must not throw butter at Miss Boyle.' "

Walking back down the darkened corridors, in which only a few seniors lounged about, Jane thought that what was really wrong with Miss Boyle was that she was out-of-date. This alone would make Mr. Charrington take her away. She didn't mind missing the games at all, except that a large moon rocket was going to be launched during them and this she had wanted to see. She was quite determined not to do any lines.

All this she explained to Jemima when she got back to the dormitory. Everyone else was asleep, and the two little girls whispered together excitedly. Jemima said Jane was very lucky not to be beaten and really quite lucky to miss the Highland Games, though she agreed it was sad to miss the rocket. But when she heard about Jane running away, she became very serious. She begged her not to and said Jane would certainly be caught, and then Miss Boyle would really beat her into tiny pieces and possibly expel her. Jane said she thought this most unlikely, but agreed to think about it. Secretly, however, she decided that by the same time next day she would be far from Scotland.

By the time the early-morning bell rang at six o'clock it was real Peeg weather. Thick fog covered the island, and a strong cold wind blew straight from the mainland (coming in the first place from Siberia, as the geography mistress had explained) and moaned through the pines and round the goal posts on the lacrosse fields. But the Glenelg Games took place whatever the weather. Indeed, Miss Boyle had said, while teaching the senior girls how to "flight" a caber with the wind, that the worse the weather the better. "The Highland Games are a test of skill," she said, "not mere brute strength."

The whole school hurried through breakfast and then out onto the gravel sweep in front of the front door. Four buses were to take them, the teachers, and all the domestic staff to Glenelg, forty miles away.

Only Jane and old Macmillan were left behind. Jane to do her lines, Macmillan because he was ninety-two and had to look after his boiler. "He will also keep an eye on you," said Miss Boyle.

Ten minutes later Jane was standing at the window of the First Form classroom, watching the buses disappear. She heard a door banging down one of the gloomy corridors. She began to feel very small and alone, and quite unlike even leaving the classroom, much less running away from school.

She felt even more alone a quarter of an hour later when old Macmillan stumped in and said he was off. "I havenny missed one of the Heeland Games fey eighty years," he said, "and ame noo changing me customes noo."

Shortly after, he left in a small black car covered with dents. Now Jane was the only person on the Island of Peeg. And suddenly she began to feel rather frightened. As the wind rattled the windows and the fog wrapped itself closer and closer round the house, she remembered the ghost stories they used to tell each other after lights-out in the dormitory. How one girl had felt a cold hand on her neck down by the locker room one night; about the unearthly screeching heard coming from the music rooms. On tiptoe, Jane moved to the door and very quietly turned the key in the lock. Obviously she couldn't run away today. She would stay quietly in the First Form classroom and not move an inch.

She was just beginning to feel calmer and safer when her eye was caught by the handle of the door. It was moving.

Someone—or something—was turning it very slowly, trying to get in. Jane was rooted to the spot. She said afterward that her hair had stood completely on end and she had felt her heart stop beating. And that, when the door was suddenly shaken and a strange high, quavery voice wailed "Whooooooooo," she had almost fainted.

There was dead silence. The wind moaned in the chimney. Then the door shook violently again—"Whooooooooo." As though sleepwalking, Jane began to move very quietly toward the door. Once more it rattled; once more the eerie voice cried "Whooooooooo." Then, shaking with fear, Jane turned the key, pulled the door open, and stared into the long corridor outside.

Standing there, her long fair hair rather wild, her face tearstained, stood Jemima Garing.

"Jemima!"

"Jane!"

The two little girls flung their arms round each other and kissed and hugged and excitedly explained. Jemima had decided that if Jane was going to run away, then she would run away too. She had slipped off the bus after her name had been checked and hidden round by the kitchens. Then, walking through the empty school looking for Jane, she had become more and more frightened. The locked First Form classroom and the silence had been the last straw. Especially the silence.

"Why didn't you *answer?*" said Jemima.

"I was rooted to the spot," said Jane.

She did not say, however, that she had decided not to run away. Jemima was a sweet and gentle girl who, though sometimes surprisingly daring, was usually more timid than Jane. That was one reason Jane liked her. But she had been very impressed by Jemima slipping off the bus and then walking all through the empty school, and she didn't want to admit that she had been too frightened even to leave the classroom, much less run away.

In any case, now that Jemima was with her, she decided they could run away after all.

"First," said Jane, "we must go to the kitchen and collect enough food for our journey. Then get a map, mackintoshes, warm clothes, torches, et cetera."

Giggling and shouting, they hurried down to the kitchens. Jane's plan was to borrow two bicycles and go to the nearest railway station, at Blair, thirty-five miles away. This would take them a day. They would catch the first train to Aldeburgh and, with all the changes, this would take them another day. To last them for two days they packed a loaf of bread, a pound of butter, four pints of milk, twenty-four slices of ham, and some bars of chocolate. Jane thought that the larder seemed extraordinarily empty for so large a school, but then she remembered that it was Saturday, the day when the food arrived from the mainland, and that Miss Boyle, among other ideas about food, was always determined there should be no waste.

They soon finished packing and then dressed themselves warmly in jeans, sweaters, thick socks, and gum boots. They were hurrying along to Miss Boyle's study to see what money they could borrow when Jemima, who was a little way behind, suddenly called out, "I think I can hear a car coming up the drive."

It was true. Leaning out of the window, they could hear the muffled sound of an engine coming through the fog. The car seemed to be moving very slowly and every few seconds blew its horn. Before long they could see headlights and then the vague outline of its shape.

It was a Land Rover. And as it came slowly closer, it became more and more familiar. It had a streak of white paint that Jane recognized on the bonnet; there was a dent that she remembered in one of the back mudguards; and when it stopped and Jane could see that its number was LLJ560F, there could no longer be any doubt.

"It's Mummy and Daddy," she shouted. "It's our Land Rover." And followed by Jemima she ran down the corridor to the main stairs.

They arrived at the front door as the big knocker was banged twice. Jane undid the bolts, turned the heavy handle, and pulled the door open.

There, standing in the fog, a huge tartan scarf wrapped several times round her throat, stood Mrs. Deal.

"Well, what a piece of luck," said Mrs. Deal. "Fancy you opening the door yourself, Miss Jane. I was quite prepared for a man or a stranger."

"What are you doing here, Mrs. Deal?" said Jane, amazed. "I thought it was Mummy and Daddy. I didn't know you could drive."

"There's a lot you don't know about me," said Mrs. Deal. "Indeed I can drive. Now let's get in out of the wind."

The wind was now so strong that it was quite difficult to get the door shut. When they had done so, Mrs. Deal took off her large leather gloves and unwrapped the long scarf. She was quite a small woman, with bright eyes, graying hair tied into a bun on the back of her head from which the hair was always getting loose, and a passion for dusting and cleaning.

Looking at this short, neat figure, which she had now learned could drive, Jane suddenly found herself thinking how much warmer and easier and cheaper it would be to run away in the Land Rover.

"And who's your friend?" said Mrs. Deal.

"Jemima Garing," said Jane absently. Somehow they

must get Mrs. Deal on their side or else trick her into taking them to the station.

"Pleased to meet you," said Mrs. Deal, holding out her
thin hand. "But it seems so quiet and empty. Where are
all the other girls? At prep?"

"No, all the other girls have escaped," said Jane without
thinking. "I mean," she said hurriedly, "have gone to the
Glenelg Highland Games. You see, there are a lot of
rather terrible things about this school which Mummy and
Daddy don't know. The thing is, Mrs. Deal, could you
help us? You see . . ."

But before she could finish, a strange and terrifying thing
happened. There was suddenly, quite close, the most tremendous explosion. For an instant the hall was lit by a
dazzling flash. And then a moment later all the windows
blew inward with a crash, scattering the floor with glass.
The lights went out, there came another, fainter explosion, and then silence, except for the wild flapping of the
long curtains and the sound of the storm outside.

The three of them stood trembling. At last Jemima
whispered, "What was it?"

"It might be blasting in the quarry," said Jane. "You
know, Jemima, opposite the causeway."

But Mrs. Deal raised her arm and said in a deep, odd
voice, "Russians!"

"How do you mean?" said Jane.

"It was the bomb," said Mrs. Deal. "I knew they'd
come. It was in the *Sunday Mirror* last Sunday. That was a
minor tactical bomb."

"Oh, I'm frightened," Jemima suddenly cried. She ran
to Mrs. Deal and seized her arm. "What shall we do?"

"We must cover ourselves in brown paper at once," said
Mrs. Deal, looking round the dark, windy hall.

"Oh, don't be silly," said Jane, whom Jemima always

made feel brave. "Why should the Russians bomb Peeg? It was probably the dynamite in the quarry blowing up. It happened last term, only not so bad. Come on, we must go and look."

She took hold of Jemima and pulled her to the door. Reluctantly, Mrs. Deal followed them both out onto the drive.

It was blowing a real storm. The fog came now thick, now thin as the wind whirled it along; the rain was lashing down in a way not even Miss Boyle would have dared call Scotch mist, and the blown pines sounded like a heavy sea.

"Quick," said Jane, running to the Land Rover. "We must go and see what's happened."

"A minor tactical bomb," repeated Mrs. Deal, remembering the *Sunday Mirror*. "Blast area half a mile." But she let herself be shoved into the driver's seat and soon, with windshield wipers swishing, they were moving slowly through the fog toward the causeway.

"At least your poor parents will be safe," said Mrs. Deal after a while.

"Why?" said Jane.

"That's why I came up here," said Mrs. Deal. "Your father thought I would soften the blow. He kindly lent me the Land Rover to take a holiday and visit my brother in Peeblesshire, but mainly so that I could tell you that he and your mother have had to go suddenly to America again for three months. They were very upset—but now, of course, it turns out for the best."

"I see," said Jane. She was sad that her mother and father had gone to America again, but they would be back soon. In fact, once she and Jemima had escaped she could fly out and join them. Except that she had no money. Also, if the council houses were shut up, where could she and Jemima stay? Jane suddenly decided that the best thing would be to take Mrs. Deal into their confidence.

"Mrs. Deal," she said, "I think I must confess something to you."

"What is it, Miss Jane?" said Mrs. Deal, slowing the car almost to a walking pace and peering into the fog, which had suddenly grown very thick. "Have you been misbehaving?"

Then Jane explained about Peeg School: about tossing the caber, about Extreme Cases and being beaten with Miss Boyle's slipper, and all the other things she was sure her mother and father would have objected to. She told Mrs. Deal about the butter and how she had decided to run away and how she hoped Mrs. Deal would help them. *"Please,* Mrs. Deal," she ended, "I know Mummy and Daddy wouldn't want me to stay here."

To her surprise, Mrs. Deal seemed scarcely interested. "Well, I can't say about all that, Miss Jane," she said. "That's not my province. You'll have to speak to Mr. and Mrs. Charrington. At the moment we must *all* try to escape. If it's the Russians on the move, which seems more and more likely every minute to me, there's no knowing where it will end. We'll make first for my brother Frank in Peeblesshire and then let him decide."

They had now nearly reached the end of the drive. But as Mrs. Deal slowly drove nearer the sea, the most extraordinary sight became clear through the fog. The waves were high and fierce, filling the air with noise. But instead of breaking against the causeway and crashing over it as usual in a storm, they now careered in uninterrupted lines between the mainland and Peeg. A jagged break in the road showed what had happened. The explosion had blown the middle of the causeway to smithereens. They were cut off.

The two little girls and Mrs. Deal stared into the fog in silence. But as they stared, Jane began to notice something even stranger. The length of the causeway had hardly been a hundred yards. Valerie McClaughlan of the Sixth Form, who could toss a caber as far as a man, had easily been able to throw a stone from shore to shore. But now even her great arm would scarcely have landed one half-way. It was almost impossible to see across to the mainland. Jane rubbed her eyes and peered out. Perhaps it was a trick of the explosion or the fog. And yet . . . Jane stared and calculated. And then suddenly—there was proof!

"Look!" cried Jane. "Look Jemima, look Mrs. Deal." Turning excitedly, she pointed to the left.

At that moment, as can happen in those parts of Scotland, the fog lifted entirely. Following Jane's finger, they looked across the rough gray sea and saw a tiny island, more like a rock, peeping round the end of the headland. It was Little Peeg, and normally it couldn't be seen at all, *normally it was only halfway up the island*.

"Do you see?" said Jane. "It's Little Peeg. And see how far we are from the shore. We're floating. We're floating away to sea."

As they watched, the little stub of rock came fully into view; a gap widened as they gradually floated past it; and then, as suddenly as it had cleared, the fog flowed round them again and everything was hidden.

"Now," said Mrs. Deal in a trembling voice, "none of us can run away, even if we wanted to. No one can escape. We're trapped."

3

THEY NEARLY DIE OF THIRST

THOUGH IT WAS not long before they found out, part of what had happened was fairly simple. The storm had not yet reached Glenelg, and the moon rocket had therefore been launched as planned. Unfortunately, it had gone off course. Rising slowly to the roaring of its motors and the oohs and aahs of fifty thousand watching people, it had suddenly started to turn to its left. The launch control officer had immediately pressed his destruction button. But a fault in transmission had delayed the explosion until the exact moment that the rocket had crashed onto the causeway between Peeg and the mainland.

As to how Peeg floated, they were also to find that out quite soon. But, naturally, it was this that surprised them most of all.

"But are you *sure* it's floating?" said Jemima, as they drove back to school through the fog. "How could a huge island made of rocks and earth float? It must weigh a million tons."

All the windows at the end of the school near the causeway had been broken by the explosion, as had many of those on the hall side. The glass, paper and dust, and general mess had completely cheered up Mrs. Deal.

"Come on, girls," she said, "you've discussed the island quite enough. I'm sure there is some quite simple explanation which we will hear on the wireless. There's so much work to do here I hardly know where to begin. Now, Jane, show me where the dusters are kept."

They worked all morning to repair the damage caused by the explosion. The electricity, of course, had been cut off with the causeway. Jane found five dozen candles but, not knowing how long it might be before they were rescued, she and Jemima decided to use them as little as possible. In the semidarkness of the storm, they swept and straightened, led by a reanimated Mrs. Deal, who had obviously decided to forget the Russians and who sometimes actually sang with pleasure, until, except for the smashed glass, you would hardly have known anything had happened.

But the broken panes caused a lot of trouble. In the end they decided to live on the far side of the school, where the windows weren't broken. They chose Miss Boyle's study for their sitting room and soon had a large fire blazing in the grate. Mrs. Deal was given Miss Boyle's bedroom, and Jane and Jemima chose a small, comfortable room nearby.

Lunchtime brought a shock. While the two girls finished moving their clothes from the First Form dormitory to their new room, Mrs. Deal went down to the kitchen to prepare the meal. Almost at once she came back.

"Jane, Jane," she said, hurrying into their bedroom, "where's the food? I've never seen such a larder in my life. It's a disgrace."

Following her down, they found that the larder, as Jane had noticed when they were preparing their picnic, was almost empty. On its long, cool marble shelves, under its seventeen wire-gauze covers, there were only four tins of sardines, four pints of milk, a loaf of bread, one dozen eggs, a pound of butter, and some sliced ham.

"We're not going to keep body and soul together on *that* for very long," said Mrs. Deal.

"There's our picnic," said Jane.

"Picnic, indeed," said Mrs. Deal. "What else? I'm not blaming you, Miss Jane." Indeed, Jane had begun to feel rather guilty. "But this is no way to run a school. Perhaps there are two larders? Or a store of tins?"

Jane said she didn't know, but suggested they all search later. They made a good lunch, sitting in the warm kitchen, of ham and fried bread and fried eggs—two each, which Jane thought rather extravagant of Mrs. Deal, considering the desperate straits they were in.

When lunch was over, Jane said, "Now I think we should all take pieces of paper and go round the school and make lists of things that might be useful in our emergency."

"I have a lot to do, Miss Jane," said Mrs. Deal. "The least we can do is to keep the school tidy and clean during our visit here."

"But we must know what we've got," said Jane. "Fishnets or food or gunpowder or even life belts and rubber rings. Supposing we started to sink. Think of that."

"Islands don't sink," said Mrs. Deal firmly, clattering and clinking knives and glasses.

"Islands don't normally float," said Jane crossly. "I would have thought once they started floating they could start sinking."

Jemima stood up and said, "You don't really think that, do you, Jane? We won't drown, will we?"

"We could easily drown," said Jane. "That's why we

must look for life belts and boats and gunpowder for making signals, et cetera. Actually, I think we are sinking a bit. I felt a definite lurch just then."

"Oh, no," cried Jemima, "oh, no. I'm so bad at swimming."

Mrs. Deal left the sink and came up to the table. "That's enough of that, Miss Jane," she said. Then, putting her arm round Jemima, she said, "Don't you worry. There's going to be no sinking on this island while I'm on it. You depend on the Royal Navy. My husband was in the Navy, and I know what I'm talking about. They'll find we've gone in the morning and come and take us off directly. And I shouldn't wonder if we didn't bump into one of the other islands before we drift much farther. Don't you worry, we'll be off here by tomorrow night. Now you two run off and make your lists. We'll meet again for an early supper at seven and then off to bed."

Despite their fear of ghosts, and even though the storm made it dark enough to use torches, Jane and Jemima decided to search separately.

In fact, Jane found that she was no longer frightened as she hurried down the dark corridor on the top floor. When Peeg House had been a school it had seemed forbidding and haunted. Now, however, they were setting out to sea. They were in the middle of a storm, which she could hear drumming on the roof and roaring through the pines. The school was their only protection. It was their only supply of food and weapons, more like a ship in which they had been wrecked, and, as she searched, Jane pretended she was Robinson Crusoe looking for things to help them in the dangers ahead.

Unfortunately, a school is not the ideal thing to be wrecked in. The two girls found very few things they thought could be of much use. Jane found twenty bars of chocolate in the girls' lockers. The games mistress had a large transistor wireless and a small fishing rod. In the geography mistress' desk she found twenty-four compasses. In Miss Boyle's bedroom cupboard she found three and a half bottles of gin, which would be useful for medical purposes.

Jemima had written down: one shed full of coal, one pile of peat outside back door, one large birthday cake in Latin mistress' room.

But the person who had done worst was Mrs. Deal. Instead of a list, she had just gathered all the brooms, dusters, tins of polish, etc., she could find. When they returned to the kitchen they found her holding a candle by her collection, counting.

"That makes ten brooms, five mops, sixteen dusters, two vacuum cleaners (which we won't be able to use, of course), eight tins of Mansion House floor polish, and six dustpans and brushes." Mrs. Deal turned to Jane. "At least there's no shortage of essential cleaning materials," she said.

"Honestly, Mrs. Deal," said Jane crossly, "don't you realize this is an emergency? For one thing, Jemima and I have found hardly any more food, so we've only enough for a few more days. We may have to try and get the butter off the dining room ceiling. Here, take your compass. You may need it."

Mrs. Deal put the compass absently into her apron pocket. "We've plenty for our purpose, Miss Jane," she said. "I'll make a nice ham omelet tonight, and we can start off with sardines on toast."

"What do you mean?" said Jane. "We must have rationing. We may not be rescued for days. Or weeks."

"Or months," said Jemima in a small voice.

"If I thought *that* I'd jump right out of that window this minute," said Mrs. Deal.

Since they were on the ground floor, Jane didn't think this meant Mrs. Deal was taking the situation very seriously. Nor was she able to persuade her that they should just have half a sardine each for their supper. But when they had finished eating, something happened which did convince Mrs. Deal that things might become more dangerous than she had supposed.

They were sitting round the fire in Miss Boyle's study. Mrs. Deal was sipping a tumbler of medicinal gin to settle her stomach. Jane and Jemima were testing their compasses. All at once the clock on the mantelpiece struck nine, and Jemima suggested they listen to the news to see if there was anything about them. Mrs. Deal turned on the games mistress' wireless, and in a minute they heard the calm voice of the announcer.

". . . extraordinary tragedy this morning. The moon probe rocket, whose flight was to be a highlight of the Glenelg Highland Games, went off course. It headed southwest, and its landing on the little Island of Peeg unfortunately seems to have coincided with the functioning of the faulty destruct mechanism. As a result, the Island of Peeg has been totally destroyed. The Island of Peeg was the site of Peeg Girls' School. Nearly all the students were fortunately at the games. The headmistress, Miss Boyle, has stated that she believes only two girls were on the island, and it is feared that they must have perished. Their names have been withheld until the next of kin have been informed. The Minister of Aviation has promised a full inquiry into the misfiring of the rocket."

After this momentous news Jemima switched off the wireless. "They think we're dead," she said.

"That certainly means they won't come and look for

us," said Jane. "Days may pass before we are rescued. Or, as Jemima said, months. Then a little ship will pull up on our rocky shore and find our poor pathetic skeletons, bleached and burned by the sun, huddled round the remnants of our last fire. Only the faltering sentences in our log will tell the sad tale of courage and suffering to a waiting world."

Mrs. Deal, who had been nervously patting her bun and sipping her gin, looked up sharply. "That will do, Miss Jane. Certainly the situation is a little more serious now, and we will have to go carefully with the food. But I've no doubt that some good ship of the Royal Navy will soon find us. We must trust to Providence and to the Royal Navy and not make matters worse by thinking gloomy thoughts." Her own face, however, became gloomier and gloomier, even though she quickly had another tumbler of medicinal gin. And when she went to bed soon afterward, forgetting to tell the two girls to go to bed as well, Jane knew she must be quite worried.

She herself was very excited and soon managed to cheer up Jemima. They sat far into the night, talking and planning. They decided they would have to hunt for food on the island. They wrote out messages to put in bottles and throw into the sea. They agreed they would like to be rescued, but not for a week at least.

However, when at last they got into bed and said good night, Jane did begin to wonder if it would be as enjoyable as she and Jemima imagined. Listening to the storm rage round the house in the darkness, she suddenly realized that the island must actually be moving. But to where? To what? Perhaps her joke was true, and if they hit an iceberg or were struck by a typhoon or cyclone or hurricane they might actually sink. Lying on her back, listening to the rain on the window, she thought she heard a new noise,

33

deeper and more menacing, like distant lions roaring in a jungle. It was in fact the sea, raised into great waves by the storm, dashing itself against the rocks and beaches all round the island. And as it washed against the cliffs, as the fierce wind swept on and on, the Island of Peeg moved slowly but steadily into the night, farther and farther out upon the wide Atlantic.

They awoke next day to find the storm blowing harder than ever. When Mrs. Deal went out to see if she could find some vegetables to make a soup, she returned almost at once, wet, breathless, her bun of hair unwound and wild. "Nearly blew me inside out," she said.

However, there was a lot to do indoors. After a breakfast of two sardines, one glass of milk, a slice of bread, a slice of the Latin mistress' birthday cake, and two slices of ham each, Jane and Jemima went out to light the boiler. Mrs. Deal took a bucket and mop up to the hall and said she would have another really hard look for food.

The boiler took all morning. It was a large iron one, like an old-fashioned train engine. Jane and Jemima made a tiny fire at the opening and then, once this was lit, they added more and more coal to it, gradually building it farther and farther back under the boiler. After two hours they had quite a good fire going and were having to feed coal onto it with long-handled shovels. Hands began to move on dials attached to various pipes. Steam hissed out of minute cracks. Thermometers rose. The boiler room grew hotter and hotter, and by the time Mrs. Deal called them for lunch their fire had grown to a furnace and its cheerful roaring filled the cellar.

For lunch they each had two more sardines (the last), two slices of ham, a glass of milk, another slice of the

Latin mistress' birthday cake, and a bar of chocolate. Mrs. Deal had failed to find any more food.

During the afternoon time began to drag. They all felt hungry, though no one mentioned it. The continuous noise of the storm began to wear them down. Every time they looked out of a window all they saw was whirling mist and streaming rain. Even feeding the boiler, which ate a tremendous lot of coal, seemed less exciting.

For supper they each had two slices of ham, two bars of chocolate, one piece of bread and butter, and a glass of milk. To save candles, they ate by the light of the ones on the Latin mistress' cake. Luckily she was, or was about to be, forty-nine.

After supper they were quite definitely hungry. Mrs. Deal wrote a long letter to her brother Frank, to be put in a bottle when the weather improved. Quite early they all had baths and then went to bed, not forgetting to turn down the boiler first.

Jane was awakened early, after a night filled with dreams about huge meals, by a really painful pang of hunger. She lay still for a while, her eyes shut, trying to get back into the last dream, which had been something about being found in a storm by some gypsies who immediately gave her plate after plate of pheasant, rabbit and onion stew, and mugs of hot, sweet tea.

But when she opened her eyes, food was forgotten. For there, at last, was the sun. Sun, pouring through the curtains and shining on the wall; sun, making the birds sing and the air smell fresh. Jane raced out of bed, woke Jemima, and together, when they had dressed, they ran down to Mrs. Deal's room. She, too, seemed excited that the storm had gone. Soon all three were hurrying out of the front door, eager to see whatever they would see.

"If we're near a passing ship or one of the West Highland islands," said Mrs. Deal, her confidence restored, "we can light a bonfire. I may even," she added grimly, "take to the water." Mrs. Deal was a very good swimmer.

The walk from the school up to where they could see the sea round the side of Mount Peeg, though it only took a quarter of an hour, was steep and boggy. But the tough, springy heather, the sponges of moss, the light, mild air, the freshness, the wetness, the excitement, made them laugh and run and forget how hungry they were. Larks rose toward the sun. Partridges whirred up and glided away down the hillside.

"We could try to catch come trout in the burn," said Jane happily.

"And there's gulls' eggs," said Jemima.

As they neared the curve of the hillside they began to run. Even Mrs. Deal urged her thin legs to a lively pace.

The sight was incredible. Gone was the islet of Little Peeg. Gone the gray lumps of big Peeg's neighbors—Eigg and Muck. Instead, a vast expanse of blue ocean, a prairie of endless waves, whipped at their tops by the brisk wind into fluffy ridges and covered in enormous rafts of foamy bubbles.

"It's lovely," said Jane. "It's like a miracle."

"Look at the waves. Look at the gulls," cried Jemima. "It's so exciting."

"It's terrible," said Mrs. Deal. "Really, Miss Jane, this is a serious situation. How we are going to inform your father and Lady, that is Mrs., Charrington, I have no idea. Now we must immediately get round the side of this hill and see if we can see what's happened to the islands and the mainland. We must pray they are not too far behind us, or I shall have to prepare myself for several hours in the water."

But another ten minutes' hard walking, after which they could see over the school and the fir wood, back to where the rest of Scotland should have been, brought no comfort. There was no sign of land or ship. Only the blue Atlantic stretching to the horizon, its great flatness dancing in the sun.

Mrs. Deal at last resigned herself.

"Well, there's nothing more we can do," she said, "except, as I said before, put our trust in Almighty Providence and the sharp eyes of the British Navy."

"It is rather odd that a huge, big island should be blown along so fast," said Jemima. "Yet it's always seemed quite real. I mean real heather and rocks and earth and things."

"It's rather odd that it should float at all," said Jane, "leaving out its speed of floating. It's definitely an odd island. We'll have to study it later. But I'm ravenously hungry. Let's go and have some breakfast."

Reminded of their hunger, they all hurried back to the school. For breakfast they each had a glass of milk (the last of the milk), one bar of chocolate, two slices of ham, two slices of bread and butter (the last of the bread and the butter), and a slice of birthday cake.

After breakfast they set out to get food. Jane fetched the fishing rod from the games mistress' room, where Jemima found a tin full of hooks and a float in the dressing table, and then they started together for the burn.

The two girls walked to a spot known as the Deep Pool. If you lay on the large rock above it and kept quite still, you would soon see the dark, submarine-shaped trout dart beneath the surface or hang in the water, their tails just waving, where the bubbles from the waterfall were thickest.

But now the burn was very full from all the rain. Jemima, who seemed to know about fishing, said, "We'll be lucky if we catch anything today. My brother says the fish can't see when the water's muddy like that. Let's get some worms."

They turned up the large, flat stones on the bank and soon had a good collection of fat and thin worms. Jemima put a piece of one of these on her hook, stood on the bank, and flicked her line into the burn just by the waterfall.

Jane sat on a rock and watched. She was rather surprised at Jemima's skill, and also a bit jealous. But when, after ten minutes, there was still no bite she began to worry again about what they would eat. But suddenly, when she was also beginning to get rather bored, the float bobbed under the water twice and then shot across the pool.

Immediately Jemima shouted, "Come and help me."

By the time Jane reached her, a huge trout (nine inches, they measured afterward) was leaping and spinning on the end of her line. Jemima seized it in her hand and with a quick yank pulled the hook out of its mouth. Then she threw the trout onto the grass behind her.

"Oh, the poor thing," said Jane.

"You're really meant to hit them on the head," said Jemima, "but I never can. They soon die. My brother says they can't really feel. Look out. I'm going to cast."

Jemima now began to catch trout much faster. She caught two more and then let Jane have a turn. But Jane twice caught her hook in the grass—and once in her finger—and when she did get it in the burn somehow, all the trout took no notice of it. So Jemima took it again, and after two hours six brown trout were scattered in the grass and they decided that was enough to take back to the school to eat.

Nor had Mrs. Deal been idle. Behind the boiler house she had found Mr. Macmillan's garden. The old Scotsman had grown a mass of uninteresting but useful vegetables, and the kitchen table was piled high with potatoes, turnips, and cabbages. These Mrs. Deal cooked and heaped round the grilled trout. For dessert, she fried the last slices of the Latin mistress' cake.

For the first time since the island had floated away they felt really full. Mrs. Deal said she thought she had the strength to start on some mopping and dusting. The two girls hurried out into the sun and spent the afternoon getting food. Jemima caught four more trout, and Jane, climbing dangerously on the cliffs, collected twenty-four gulls' eggs.

They went to bed that night, after an enormous ham omelet, with the larder full, full themselves, and all much happier. Mrs. Deal said she had a strange feeling the Royal Navy would arrive the next day.

So began four of the calmest weeks they were to know on the Island of Peeg. Each morning the sun reached a little higher in the sky as they slowly drifted, or were blown, farther south. In fact, their speed was not all that slow. Pieces of wood thrown into the sea were soon left behind. Jane and Jemima thought it must be something to do with currents, but they couldn't really understand it and decided it was just another odd thing about the island.

For the first two weeks, although there was no rain, it was quite often cloudy. But during the third week it began to get hotter and hotter. At night they took off blanket after blanket until they were lying naked under a single sheet. During the day the two girls just wore knickers, while Mrs. Deal, odd but practical, took to wearing an old bathing dress she'd found in one of Miss Boyle's cupboards.

There was a great deal of work to do. All their food had

to be caught or found. Gulls' eggs and trout were what they mainly ate, but Mrs. Deal also made nettle soup and vegetable tea. Jane made a snare out of some fishing line and managed to catch one of the island's few rabbits. Sad though it was, Mrs. Deal resolutely killed this while the two girls were out. "Needs must," she said, "and the devil take the hindermost."

Every morning and every evening water had to be hand pumped up to the roof. The boiler had to be raked out and stoked. Wood had to be collected for a bonfire in case the never arriving Royal Navy should suddenly arrive. Mrs. Deal herself, apart from cooking, had decided to spring-clean the entire school from top to bottom. "I shall hand it over in a better state than I found it, if it's the last thing I do," she said. And as it grew hotter and Mrs. Deal worked harder and faster and longer, Jane thought it probably would be the last thing she did.

They began to swim every day. And it was when they first did this, from the school's favorite swimming beach, that they noticed a curious thing. The beach was much smaller. This meant, as a terrified Jemima immediately pointed out, that Peeg had sunk. But by putting a stick in the pebbles at the highest point the waves reached, they found that the island didn't seem to be sinking any more.

They found a huge heap of old bottles in a shed by Mr. Macmillan's garden. They threw three of these a day into the sea with messages in them. The messages, except for the one which had Mrs. Deal's letter to her brother, all said:

From the Island of Peeg, Scotland
The Island of Peeg was not sunk by the moon rocket, but is floating rapidly south. Jane Charrington, Jemima Garing, and Mrs. Deal are alive

and well on it. Will the finder of this message please contact the British Government or the Royal Navy at once. Reward of £500. Signed Jane Charrington, Jemima Garing, Alice Deal.

It was Jemima who first noticed that all was not well. She came back one morning from her fishing and said, "You know, I think the burn is getting smaller."

After lunch (scrambled gulls' eggs, parsnips, spring water) she took Jane to see. There was no doubt about it. You could see the marks on the rocks showing how the level of the water had fallen at least six inches. The water was also much warmer. Nor did the level in the burn fall slowly. By the end of the same afternoon it had fallen another inch. The next morning Jemima caught two trout—there were very few left now—with her hands in a tiny pool which had become cut off from the main stream of the burn. By the next day that pool, and others, had completely dried up.

And it was now they began to notice how dry the whole of Peeg had become. No longer was there the endless trickle of water, the glistening rocks. The moss was drying and turning brown. Only the tough pines seemed unaffected by the blazing sun, which all day long poured its heat upon them.

Mrs. Deal, strong as she was, could only work for an hour before having a dip in the sea. And the two girls began to spend every minute of the day in the water, except when they were looking for food.

But matters didn't grow serious until four nights after Jemima had discovered that the burn was drying up. It had been a particularly hot day, the air quivering so hard it looked as though the sun had already succeeded in setting the island on fire. When they went to bed, Jane fell asleep almost at once, exhausted by long hours in the warm sea.

She was awakened at about one o'clock in the morning by a low rumbling. At first she thought sleepily it might be thunder, but she soon realized that it came from somewhere inside the school. She woke Jemima and they went out into the corridor to listen.

"I think it's an earthquake," whispered Jemima.

"Nothing's shaking," said Jane.

"Perhaps it's a terrible sea monster crawled out of the sea," said Jemima.

"Nonsense," said Jane, beginning to feel quite brave. "We must go and look."

They put on some clothes and then set off hand in hand down the corridor. All round them the house was silent and warm, dimly lit by the large moon; the lines of dormitory beds, still neatly made as the girls had left them on the morning of the Glenelg Highland Games, had teddies and dolls by their pillows. The sea was gently swelling and murmuring in the distance. Jane began to feel less brave.

As they drew closer the rumbling became more of a jumping clank. At first they thought it was in the kitchen, but when they slowly and nervously peered round the door, it was as usual: hot from the stoves, and the floor, by Jemima's torch, covered in scuttling cockroaches. The noise, however, was now very loud; not only the sound of straining, banging metal, but loud hisses.

"I know what it is," said Jane. "Quick. The back door."

As they came out into the backyard, she saw at once that she had been right. Against the darkness of the outhouses they could see a great cloud of steam gushing from the door next to the coal cellar. From the door, too, came

42

a deafening thumping and clanging, a whistling, roaring, trembling din which seemed to shake the ground they stood on.

It was the boiler. Crawling on their hands and knees to avoid the billows of boiling steam, the two girls reached the door and looked in.

The most extraordinary sight met their eyes. The boiler itself was red-hot all over (they found afterward that Jemima, whose turn it had been to stoke it, had left the damper jammed open with a shovel). Each nut and bolt on it glowed fiercely in the dark, and its curving iron sides were in places almost white with the heat from the furnace roaring underneath. But the noise they had heard came from the huge hot-water cylinder above the boiler. The ever increasing heat of the fire had made the water in the cylinder boil; then the pressure of steam had blown out the safety valves and started the cylinder jumping. Now, to the sound of furious but muffled bubbling from inside, the vast iron object, encased in white plaster, was leaping up and down on its supports, shaking off great white chunks, loosing piercing jets of steam from safety valves and other vents, and looking every second as though it would wrench itself away from its pipes and its platform and come crashing down onto the red-hot boiler beneath.

They crawled backward and then ran to the kitchen. "You turn on all the hot taps, then come and help me get the fire extinguishers," shouted Jane.

The fire extinguishers were scattered about the school. Jane collected one from the hall and another from outside the geography room. On the way back she met Jemima.

"It's extraordinary," Jemima said. "I've turned on all the hot taps in the kitchen and the pantry, and all that comes out is steam."

"She'll blow up soon," said Jane, remembering a film she'd seen where boilers were called "she." "Here, take this extinguisher."

They ran back and were soon crouched before the boiler. By the glow, Jane read the instructions: "Strike knob sharply with both hands. Then direct nozzle at fire."

Jemima leaned over the cylinder and banged her hands on the knob. Jane shielded her face and directed the nozzle at the boiler.

For a moment nothing happened. Then it jerked in her hand, there was a gentle *whoosh*, and a great cloud of white foam shot from the nozzle.

"Come on," shouted Jane. "It's fun."

Six times they had to run back to fetch a new extinguisher. But at last the fire was out, the cylinder stopped leaping, and the boiler room, though several feet deep in white foam, seemed safe to leave. Wearily the two girls returned to the school. As they trudged through the kitchen they could hear steam still gushing from the hot taps. Without even bothering to wash off the dirt and extinguisher foam, they got into bed and immediately fell asleep.

But it was Mrs. Deal who discovered the true meaning of the boiler incident. When they came down to breakfast she was sitting gloomily in front of a dozen gulls' eggs.

"I don't know what you girls were doing last night," she said. "I won't speak of the mess in the boiler room. You must have gone mad. A week's work there would be a conservative estimate. But you've run the tank dry, and there's no water in the well."

"No water?" said Jane.

"No water," said Mrs. Deal. "I shall have to do the scrubbing with seawater. It's almost unheard-of."

Jane and Jemima explained how the boiler had nearly blown up, and Mrs. Deal then agreed that they had done very well.

After a somewhat drying breakfast of salty flatfish Jemima had caught in the sea and some thick scrambled gulls' eggs, the two girls set off with buckets to get water from the burn.

The burn was dry.

"But it can't be," said Jane. "Surely it wasn't dry yesterday."

"I didn't go yesterday," said Jemima.

"Let's walk down," said Jane. "There's bound to be some water left in one of the pools."

But it was the same down the whole of the winding, tumbling course. The smooth rocks, the thickly scattered stones were white in the sun and almost too hot to touch; already, between them, the mud was starting to crack. Even worse, as they walked slowly toward the sea, was the smell of dead trout. There were few of these left from Jemima's fishing, but as the burn had dried those that remained had floundered down to the deeper pools. When these had evaporated, the trout had died.

The two girls stared horrified at this unpleasant scene. At last Jane said, "We must get back to Mrs. Deal. We must plan. This is a real emergency."

"Well, at least we won't starve," said Jemima. "There's plenty of gulls' eggs still, and I can catch fish in the sea."

"Yes, but being thirsty is quite different," said Jane. "You say 'starving,' but you don't say 'thirsting'; you say 'dying of thirst'; it's much more serious. You can only live a few days without water."

Mrs. Deal either rose to occasions or sank beneath them. Now she chose to sink. When Jane and Jemima told her about the burn, she sat abruptly down.

"Well, that's that then," she said. "The End. It's been a long life and a gloomy one, but I won't say I shan't be sorry to go. I *shall* be sorry to go. Until our time comes we'd best keep on as normal. You two girls go and make your beds while I make a start on the boiler room."

After lunch, which was already difficult to eat, Jane and Jemima decided to go and look for water. They took umbrellas to shield them from the fierce sun, but even with these they were soon forced to turn back. The heat was so great that they felt they were being dried in front of a fire. The peaty earth of Peeg was cracked and baked, the heather and grass shriveled brown. "We'll go out at night when it's cooler," said Jane.

They spent the rest of the afternoon lying exhausted in Miss Boyle's hot armchairs, listening to the wireless. Apart from a lot of crackles, they could only get faint African music and, since Jane had noticed from her compass that they had never stopped moving south, she decided that they were probably near the equator.

For supper Mrs. Deal gave them bowls of raw gulls' eggs as the most liquid thing they had. But their throats were beginning to swell, and they could only swallow a few mouthfuls.

It grew dark, as Jane said, with tropical suddenness, but hardly any cooler. When the two girls went out to look for water it was still like walking in a large, uneven oven.

Their search for water was no more successful than during the day. They walked slowly up the side of Mount Peeg to the springs which had supplied the burn, but they were all dry. Then they walked out to the low, forty-foot cliffs at the front of the island. The tiny streams that had once oozed and trickled from hundreds of places had all disappeared.

They even climbed down to the beach. Here it was

Jemima who noticed something rather odd. She threw an old piece of driftwood into the calm water, but instead of slowly being left behind by the island, as would have happened before, it just floated there, unmoving.

"Even the current has stopped carrying us," whispered Jemima.

They arrived back at the school exhausted. "We're getting weaker," said Jane, as they stood panting in the kitchen.

"Look, even the cockroaches are thirsty," said Jemima. In their search for moisture they seemed to have lost all fear; the moonlit floor was alive with the crunchy beetles.

Jane spent a restless night. Several times she dreamed she was on fire and was then blissfully put out by a huge hose spouting water. Twice she was awakened by what she thought was a gentle rain pattering on the window, only to find it was Jemima snoring.

The next two days were a nightmare. They all felt too thirsty to eat, and so weak that it was a long time before they managed to get out of bed. Each day the sun blazed its way across the huge steely sky and not a breath of wind moved on the Atlantic. They lay about, dozed, occasionally talked with swollen lips, fanned each other; afterward, those two days were all jumbled and confused in Jane's mind.

Toward the evening of the fourth day without water Jemima grew feverish. Hot as they all were, it was plain that she had grown even hotter. Her cheeks were flushed and there was a black rim to her lips. She suddenly burst into tears and fell on her bed calling for her mother.

"Mummy, Mummy," she cried, "why have you left me?" Then she fell into a sort of daze, lying with her eyes open, muttering and crying.

Mrs. Deal put her to bed and then sat soothing and

fanning her. "Poor child," she said. "It's no more than we can expect."

Night fell. Jane lay listening to Jemima's muttering and the *swish, swish* of Mrs. Deal's magazine fanning. She tossed and dozed, woke up and heard Jemima again, dozed and tossed. Her tongue was swelling. She thought she was back at Curl Castle, swimming in the river. She felt she was flying in a cool wind over endless fields of snow. She was in a garden at night. Suddenly it began to rain. Huge, cool drops as big as pigeons' eggs falling and bursting in her mouth. All at once she woke up again. Jemima was still muttering. By the pale light of the moon she saw that Mrs. Deal had fallen back against the wall and was asleep.

And then, deep within her, like a secret, angry determination to do something, even though she had been told not to, she felt she must fight for them all. If they went on lying there another day they would all be dead. There must be a way out.

She put her feet on the floor and stood up weakly. She walked down the corridor slowly so as to save her strength.

Outside it was very hot and very quiet. The moon was high in the cloudless sky, making the landscape of Peeg soft and sinister with its pale light. Jane walked away from the school, up the hill toward the front of the island.

The dead grass rustled as she walked. But this was the only noise. Even the ocean had fallen silent as though waiting for them to die. It stretched away all round the island, miles and miles of wrinkled, moonlit water, peaceful at Jane's feet. She walked a little way along the clifftop and then climbed down a steep pathway which led to a narrow beach.

Here the silence was even stranger. The water hardly lapped the rocks. Jane suddenly felt how frightening it was to be floating in such deep water. What lay underneath, down in those dark, cold fathoms below them?

Suddenly, she heard a noise, loud in the silence. It came from her left, a faint chink. Jane felt gooseflesh in spite of the heat. Very slowly she turned her head.

From about thirty yards away, a man was creeping toward her. Though he was bending forward, Jane saw he was quite tall. The moon caught his white hair.

As she stared he stopped and stood up. "Don't move," he said. "I have a gun."

Jane tried to speak. Her dry tongue filled her mouth; her cracked lips were open.

"Advance and be recognized," said the man. "I don't wish to shoot, but there's a war on."

Jane suddenly felt she was going to be sick. The sea tilted toward her and then sank back. She raised her arms, took one weak step forward, and then, with a low, hoarse cry, fainted onto the stones.

4

THE MYSTERY OF PEEG
EXPLAINED

WHEN JANE FELL, the tall man continued to move slowly and warily toward her, his revolver still pointed at her body. But once he was sure she was really unconscious, he put the gun back in his pocket and lifted her gently onto his huge shoulders. He turned and crunched back up the shingle until he reached some large slabs of rock which were leaning upright against each other. Moving round these, the man stopped at the side of a particularly large one which was half embedded in the cliff. Reaching forward and bending down, he felt round the edges of this until suddenly there was a faint click and the rock swung slowly open. The moonlight was just strong enough to show steep stone steps going up and into the cliff. The man stepped calmly through, Jane still hanging over his shoulder, and the rock door shut behind them.

Back at Peeg School, the heat seemed to be growing greater, not lessening as it did sometimes toward morning. Mrs. Deal had awakened at three o'clock. She saw almost at once that Jane had gone, but was too weak even to mind. "Soon we shall all be gone," she thought to herself. "Oh, lads, you come too late; oh, Admiral, where are your longboats now?" She felt her mind becoming feverish as Jemima's had been. Now that she was going to die, she thought more and more about the Navy, in which Mr. Deal had served until his own end so long ago. "Lower away, bosun," said the voice in her head; "Mr. Mate, get a tackle on that body there. Pipe it aboard, sir, pipe it aboard." Jemima had fallen asleep. Her lips were quite black. Mrs. Deal lifted her magazine and weakly tried to fan her burning forehead. "Captain's compliments, Mr. Mate. The funeral is to be with full naval honors—burial at sea."

Someone was pouring water gently between Jane's lips. She knew it wasn't a dream because it was too real and cool; at the same time, she didn't open her eyes because she feared that if she did it would stop, as it had so often before when it had really been a dream.

A voice said, "That will do, Sergeant. It says in the Manual, 'Dehydration must be treated with care. Six to eight ounces of fluid every ten minutes.' "

"Very good, sir." The water stopped. Jane opened her eyes. A thick gray beard waved just in front of her face. "That's better; that be a sight better," said the beard. "She's coming round, sir."

The beard moved, and Jane saw that it belonged to a short, bald man of about sixty, dressed in shorts, khaki shirt, and a peaked cap. His face and hands, she noticed, were quite amazingly white.

She was lying on a sofa in a long, low room, lit by electric lights with faded shades. There were photographs in frames on the walls, some tables with magazines on them,

and several armchairs. In one of these sat the man she had seen creeping toward her along the beach.

"Can I have some more water, please?" she asked him.

"I'm sorry, young lady," he said in a deep, but brisk voice, "the Manual's instructions are quite clear. Six to eight ounces every ten minutes. You can have some more in six minutes.

"Meanwhile, let me introduce us. This is Sergeant Cobbin; I am Captain Thomson. Both of the Seventh Hussars, seconded for the duration to Operation Peeg."

"I'm Jane Charrington," said Jane, her voice still very weak.

"How do you do," said Captain Thomson. He stood up—and Jane noticed how incredibly white his skin was too—and came over to her sofa. "I'm afraid I'll have to interrogate you properly later, as you probably realize. But now tell me, are you alone?"

"Alone!" cried Jane, remembering with a guilty rush the reason for her journey. "Oh, how could I have forgotten? No—quick, you must rush to Peeg School at once with water. Jemima may be dead. You must save Mrs. Deal and Jemima."

But Captain Thomson bent his tall frame swiftly forward over her and then turned hurriedly to the Sergeant. "Jemima? Mrs. Deal? These sound like code names. Has there been infiltration? Mrs. Deal Platoon? Battalion Jemima?"

"I doubt it, sir," said Sergeant Cobbin in his comforting Suffolk voice. "They sound real enough names to me. No doubt the young lady's companions."

"At all events a situation to be investigated," said Captain Thomson, marching swiftly about the room. "Get those water cans, Sergeant. And you, Miss Jane, I must warn you, if Mrs. Deal Platoon gives trouble—then short shrift. Short shrift. You may have one glass of water every ten minutes." Captain Thomson then strode from the room, beckoning Sergeant Cobbin to follow him.

Jane waited a moment till their footsteps died away, then hurried to the jug and poured herself some water, one, two, three, *four* glasses. So wonderful did it feel, cooling and soothing her dry throat, her swollen lips, that she quite ignored the Captain's instructions. Luckily, these were for people actually dying of thirst, and although she finished the entire jug it did her no harm at all. She pulled herself back to the sofa and immediately fell into a deep sleep.

Jane slept for six hours. She missed the return of Sergeant Cobbin and Captain Thomson carrying the unconscious bodies of her friends. Mrs. Deal had still been conscious when they had found her, but at the sight of Sergeant Cobbin's beard she had risen shakily to her feet and with a loud cry, "The Navy!" had fainted into his arms. She missed the careful forcing of water between Jemima's cracked and blackened lips, the gentle bathing of her forehead. By the time Jane awoke it was morning (though no daylight entered what Captain Thomson had called the anteroom), and she already felt much better.

That was the strange thing about thirst. Although they had nearly died of it in four days, once they could drink again they recovered almost at once. By that same evening Jemima was sitting up and talking, and Jane and Mrs. Deal felt almost normal.

They were all three sitting talking in the anteroom when the two soldiers came in to join them.

Captain Thomson said, "Ladies, I feel we should have a conference. We have avoided asking you disturbing questions after your terrible experience, but, as you can imagine, the Sergeant and myself are simply burning with curiosity to know about the progress of the war. We also need to know how you got involved in Operation Peeg, though it is evident you got involved by mistake. Now, Sergeant, you ask the big question."

"Well, it's the war," said Sergeant Cobbin, tugging at his beard and showing, for him, signs of excitement. "You be the first real news we've had for thirty-two years."

"Thirty-two years?" said Jane, amazed. "What war are you talking about?"

"Why, The War," said Sergeant Cobbin. "The *War*. The war that started in 1939."

"Good heavens," cried Captain Thomson, springing impatiently to his feet. "The War! The War! The War!"

So Jane and Jemima and Mrs. Deal began to learn the extraordinary story of the two old soldiers. It would take too long to tell it in their own words, but made much shorter, it was this:

At the very beginning of the Second World War, Winston Churchill had decided that the Island of Peeg would be one of his secret weapons. The idea was simple, but amazing. It had long been known that Peeg was a volcanic island; what few knew was that it was one of those rare volcanic islands which, while ordinary granite, earth, and heather on the surface, consisted inside almost entirely of soft pumice stone. *And, of course, pure pumice stone floats.*

One of the few people who knew about Peeg was Winston Churchill, who had often explored those parts when a boy. He also knew that at the far end of the island the sea had scooped an immense cavern out of the soft pumice stone, the entrance to which was out of sight below the water.

Churchill's plan was to enlarge the cavern and fill it with an enormous amount of high explosive. Large buoyancy tanks would be attached all round the island, an engine room would be built at the back by the causeway, and the causeway itself would be mined with explosive. Then, at a suitable moment, the causeway would be blown up. The island, Churchill hoped, would be jolted free of the mainland, float out to sea, and could be slowly steered to some position where its destruction would most harm the enemy. If it did not float away, then all that would have been done was to destroy the causeway; the Island of Peeg would remain as an excellent storeplace of high explosive, invaluable for resistance if Great Britain lost the war.

All but the last part of the experiment was carried out. For two years an army of fifty workers, sworn to secrecy, toiled on the island. The huge cavern was made even larger and eight million tons of TNT stored in it. Vast buoyancy tanks were attached at regular intervals round the island some forty feet below the level of the sea. An engine room was built about seventy yards from the causeway. In 1942 Captain Thomson and Sergeant Cobbin, then aged thirty-two and thirty, were moved into their quarters, which had been hollowed out of the pumice stone three-quarters of the way up the cavern. Captain Thomson, as well as being an excellent soldier, was an amateur geologist who knew a lot about rocks; Sergeant Cobbin was an engineer who had also had lessons in explosives.

Two days after they moved in, the workers moved out. Unfortunately, the train which was carrying them south was hit by a large bomb, and everyone in it was killed. This much was known to Captain Thomson and Sergeant Cobbin. But the day after that their wireless, the only link they were allowed with the mainland, was irreparably destroyed by a fall of rock. Their instructions had been very strict—on no account were they to contact anyone. They would be called on when they were needed. And for thirty-two years no one had called on them.

For thirty-two years Captain Thomson and Sergeant Cobbin had waited to serve their country. Then the moon rocket at Glenelg had crashed onto the causeway and—proving Churchill right—set Peeg upon her course. To Captain Thomson and Sergeant Cobbin—who still thought the war was going on—it seemed as though their task had at last begun.

To persuade them that the war was, in fact, over was the first thing that Mrs. Deal and the two girls tried, gently, to do. It was extremely difficult, and for a long time Captain Thomson and Sergeant Cobbin refused to believe it. In the end Jane remembered that there were a lot of old newspapers in the Fifth Form common room used in current affairs classes. These, though they didn't mention the war at all, being only one or two years old, did finally convince them. Indeed, it was just because they didn't mention the war at all that they were so convincing.

"And you say it ended in *1945?*" said Captain Thomson. "Twenty-nine years ago?" It had been a great shock to them both.

"I can't rightly get used to the idea," said Sergeant Cobbin. "You say we won? Well, that's good. That's what we hoped. But there were we, thinking them Germans had overrun the country and that stout resistance was going on in the ditches and the hedges as Winston had foretold."

"No doubt," said Captain Thomson sadly, "no doubt in the excitement of victory, they just forgot Operation Peeg."

"Oh, surely not," said Jane. "I'm sure you weren't forgotten."

"I expect a flying bomb hit some government building and destroyed everything about you," said Mrs. Deal, little knowing how accurate she was.

Captain Thomson brightened. "That's true," he said. "And in that case perhaps there's some honor in having stuck to our post through the years."

"Indeed there is," said Mrs. Deal, "a great deal of honor. You have stood by your post through thick and thin, at great personal inconvenience, in a way which adds glory and luster to the great name of the British Navy."

"Army, ma'am, Army," said Captain Thomson.

"Army, Navy, Air Force—all men at arms," said Mrs. Deal, looking quite flushed. "What does it matter? We're afloat now. To me, you'll always represent the *spirit* of the British Navy in the glorious *uniform* of the British Army."

"Hurrah!" cried Jemima from her sofa.

"Sergeant—salute!" cried Captain Thomson. And as he and Sergeant Cobbin leaped to attention and saluted, Jemima and Jane shouted "Hurrah," and Mrs. Deal, overcome with emotion, sprang to her feet and saluted too.

However, apart from a few moments like these, they all had a great deal to ask each other.

"But what did you eat?" said Jane.

"Well, we had a special arrangement with a shop in Dunlaig," said Captain Thomson. "They were to leave certain supplies at the end of the causeway every week. We collected at night. They weren't told who it was for and were paid by the government. If a bomb did destroy our records in London, no one remembered to stop that. Also, we have two and a half years' supply of tinned food stored here. There's plenty of water, of course. Two hundred thousand gallons of fuel oil for the engines."

"Supplies of drink are running low, sir," put in Sergeant Cobbin.

58

"Perfectly true, Sergeant," said Captain Thomson, "perfectly true. We're down to a crate or two of rum as I remember."

"We've got one bottle of medicinal gin left you can have," said Jane.

"Very good of you," said Captain Thomson, bowing politely to her.

"I must say," said Mrs. Deal, "I feel I would have *felt* the war had ended. Did you not feel it in your bones?"

"My *bones?*" said Captain Thomson thoughtfully. "Bones? Can't say I did."

"You see, ma'am, our instructions on that point were very strict," said Sergeant Cobbin. "We were only to come out at night, talk to no one, see no one. All orders were to come over the wireless. Unfortunately, as the Captain told you, a chunk of old rock fell on that shortly after we moved in. But I reckoned how, as we didn't answer or send any signals, they'd have guessed about that and got any orders to us by other means."

"And you must remember," said Captain Thomson, "that in the event of defeat we were to be more secret than ever."

"But thirty-five years!" said Mrs. Deal. "Well, that's a lot of time for a war—thirty-five years."

"Not at all," said Captain Thomson. "If you'll excuse me contradicting you, ma'am, there was the Peloponnesian War—at 431 B.C. to 404 B.C., very nearly twenty-seven years. The Wars of the Roses—1455 to 1487. The Crusades. It can all be gleaned from my encyclopedia of famous painters."

"There's the Thirty Years' War and the Hundred Years' War," said Jemima, whose best subject was history.

"We were ready to stay here till we died," said Sergeant Cobbin in a comfortable voice.

"Brave men!" said Mrs. Deal, flushing again.

Jane wanted to know what they had done all the time and if they hadn't been bored.

This amused Captain Thomson a great deal. "Bored?" he said in his deep, quick voice. "Oh, no; oh, dear me, no. This is a Military Establishment, run on Military lines. Of course, the Sergeant and I have relaxed discipline a little. That's inevitable in the circumstances. But besides Parades, Orders, Mess Nights, Weapon Training, we've had a great deal of work to do." And then he began to describe what he and Sergeant Cobbin had done over the years.

They had decided that the more of the island that blew up, the more effective it would be as a bomb. They had therefore dug long tunnels through the pumice stone, which now reached to every part of the island. At regular intervals they had dug little rooms off these tunnels; each room was packed with high explosive.

"Isn't it very dangerous?" said Jane.

"Very," said Captain Thomson. "Luckily, I don't smoke, and Sergeant Cobbin only likes an occasional pipe. A dust explosion is our main worry."

"Dust?" said Mrs. Deal. "You have problems with your dusting?"

"Now that we are getting older, the dusting certainly becomes no easier," said Captain Thomson.

"I think I may be able to help," said Mrs. Deal. "Let me see, we have ten brooms, five mops, six dustpans and brushes, and sixteen dusters. Yes, I've no doubt I can help with the cleaning."

"If you'll excuse me asking," said Jane, "how old are you both?"

"Not at all," said Captain Thomson. "I am sixty-four. Sergeant Cobbin is sixty-two."

He went on to explain how there had been the buoyancy tanks to inspect and the engines to keep well oiled. "We started these after Peeg was launched," said Captain Thomson. "Unfortunately, the explosion bent the propeller shaft and made steering difficult, but we headed south because I had an instinct that's where they'd want us. Then, two days ago, something went wrong with the engine and we stopped."

There had been many other things to do. Captain Thomson had collected many interesting rocks and fossils and was writing a book about them. He was also interested in art and had been studying an *Encyclopedia of 2000 Famous Painters*. "Know the thing off by heart," he said. There had been clothes to mend, a task, Jane noticed, which they could not have found very easy; both their uniforms were covered with large odd-shaped patches, clumsily stitched. They had enlarged their rooms, adding another bedroom, a shooting range, a map room, and building a staircase from the Blowup Room to the cliff. And Sergeant Cobbin had frequently studied the aeroplane they had been given. This was in special collapsible form and was an idea of Winston Churchill's so that when the island was exploded they could fly away to safety. Unfortunately, there was not room to make it in the anteroom. On warm nights they had gone out onto the narrow beach, and while Sergeant Cobbin had smoked a pipe, Captain Thomson had done some fishing; often they had just sat and looked at the lights twinkling on the shore and wondered how the war was going and when the time would come for them to be of use.

"No war," said Sergeant Cobbin sadly. "That's going to take a while to get accustomed to."

"We'll get used to it," said Captain Thomson briskly. "Military discipline, Sergeant. We've got used to a good many things together.

"But in answer to your question, Miss Charrington. We were never bored. We kept busy. That may not be the secret of happiness, but it's the secret of not being bored."

Everyone was silent. Jane still had several questions to ask, but it was now quite late in the evening of the second day after their rescue. Jane and Mrs. Deal and particularly Jemima still felt weak, and the two old soldiers were obviously still worried, despite Captain Thomson's briskness, by there being no war. So after a quick supper from the store of tins, consisting of dried egg and powdered potato, they all went to bed.

Next morning when they woke up even Jemima felt well. Captain Thomson asked them to stay as long as they liked in what he called "the Mess" (though it was in fact, as Jane pointed out, exceptionally tidy). However, they decided they would sleep in the school and just have meals with the soldiers.

"It's not that we haven't enjoyed sleeping here," Jemima said, "but it is rather strange sleeping underground."

"That's just what I wanted to ask," said Jane. "Didn't you long to see the sun sometimes?"

"Well, I did miss the sun at first, that's certainly true— did I not, sir?" said Sergeant Cobbin.

"You did," said Captain Thomson. "For the first five years you did. The Sergeant really wanted to be an airman," he went on, turning to Mrs. Deal. "That's why he spent so much time checking over the aeroplane Special Kit."

"Fancy," said Mrs. Deal. "I'd have said the Sergeant had more of a naval aspect with that beard. The air? Well, naturally he'd miss it in that case—and all that goes with it."

"Whereas the Captain here," said Sergeant Cobbin in

his calm way, "never minded a jot, did you, sir? Never so much as noticed one way or the other."

"I wouldn't say I never *noticed*," said Captain Thomson rather irritably. "I'd have been a buffoon not to notice. I put up with it, that's all. And we must now learn to get used to daylight again, Sergeant. Now the war's over we must start to adapt to a surface life.

"Nevertheless, madam," he said to Mrs. Deal, "I think we won't come with you. You will have noticed that our skins are a little pale. We must take it slowly."

"There is that tunnel, sir, we dug, what was it? Nineteen fifty or thereabouts. Comes out in the boiler room," said Sergeant Cobbin.

"So there is. Well, we may come and meet you. But lunch here, in the Mess, one o'clock sharp."

It was wonderful to get out into the air again. Although it was not exactly fresh—indeed it felt hotter than ever—it was refreshing to see the sparkling waves and be able to run and jump as much as they wanted to again.

They were just about to go down past Mount Peeg to the school when Jemima, turning to see how far behind Mrs. Deal had got, noticed a strange dark line, far away, stretching the length of the horizon. "What's that?" she said.

"I think it must be a storm," said Jane after a moment. "We'd better be quick and do what we've got to do before it reaches us."

Quite what it was they had to do none of them knew. There was something depressing about the school, stifling in the heat. Cockroaches lay on their backs, dead of thirst; also two rats. And their bedrooms reminded them how they, too, had nearly died. Mrs. Deal only had one task, which was to collect the brooms and mops and dusters.

On their way back to lunch Jane said, "Let's sleep in the

Mess after all, Mrs. Deal. Captain Thomson and Sergeant Cobbin are so nice. Also, it was so cool there."

"A good idea, Miss Jane," said Mrs. Deal. "I felt quite rude refusing. I'll say we've changed our minds."

When they could see the sea again, Jane pointed to the horizon. "It definitely is a storm," she said, "and it's getting nearer." The thin black line had now grown until it was a thick band along the horizon. Already, it was a little menacing.

Captain Thomson and Sergeant Cobbin were delighted they were going to sleep in the Mess.

"Guests at Operation Peeg after all these years, Sergeant," said Captain Thomson. "The two young ladies can have the map room, and I'll give up *my* room to Mrs. Deal."

"I shall give up *my* room to Mrs. Deal," said Sergeant Cobbin.

"Sergeant," said Captain Thomson, a flush spreading on his large white cheeks, "I said *my* room."

"And I said my room," said Sergeant Cobbin obstinately.

"Gentlemen, gentlemen," said Mrs. Deal with great pleasure. "Not on my account, pray."

The two men glared angrily at each other. Jane noticed that they had both put on new uniforms since the morning, ones that were almost unpatched.

"A compromise would be turn and turn about," said Captain Thomson. "The good lady could have my room one night and your room the next night."

"That's ridiculous," said Jane. "Think how inconvenient for poor Mrs. Deal."

"Why don't we sleep in Captain Thomson's room and Mrs. Deal in the map room," said Jemima.

"Yes," said Mrs. Deal, "I should be delighted with the map room."

"If that's what you wish, that's what I wish," said Captain Thomson gallantly. "Certainly that solves the problem. I shall sleep in the firing range."

"Oh, come, sir," said Sergeant Cobbin, "that's the most uncomfortable place on the island. There's room enough for both of us in my room. Join me."

"Well, that's very generous of you, Sergeant," said the Captain. "I shall."

After lunch Mrs. Deal and the two girls hurried back to the school to collect sheets and clothes and things like the wireless, the gin, and the compasses. If possible, it was hotter than ever, but it was a quite different heat from the days before. The air was completely still and seemed to be pressing on the island. The storm clouds reached halfway up the sky; they seemed like a lid rolling up to close over the world, and Jane thought she could hear the first faint rumblings of thunder.

Once at the school, they bustled about their tasks. They packed their clothes and Jane put the wireless and all the compasses by her case and a book of Miss Boyle's called *The Second World War*, which she thought would interest the two soldiers. Mrs. Deal made a bundle of clean sheets and also tied the mops and brooms together.

While they were all busy it grew gradually darker. The air became heavier and hotter, until Mrs. Deal and Jane, who was in the kitchen helping her, were actually dripping wet.

"Oh, please, can't we stop?" said Jane. "I want to swim. Why must we clean the ovens *now?*"

"We're almost done, Miss Jane," panted Mrs. Deal. "I'd never forgive myself if these lovely hot plates got rusty. We've been put in charge of this lovely old building, and we must not betray our trust."

Though this was hardly an accurate account of how they

came to be at Peeg School, Jane felt too hot to argue. She leaned against the sink and watched Mrs. Deal rush the wire brush up and down the long copper range. Was that thunder in the distance?

"There," said Mrs. Deal at last. "You can't leave these things a minute in the tropics."

This time it was unmistakably thunder. Much closer, it rolled toward the school. There was a faint sighing of wind, and the hot air in the kitchen moved. Then everything was still again.

"We'll collect our things and get back before the rain," said Mrs. Deal. But neither of them moved. It was as though they were waiting for something, and for no particular reason Jane began to feel nervous.

Mrs. Deal suddenly said, "Is that Miss Jemima?"

Jane listened, and then there was the sound of clattering on the kitchen stairs and a moment later Jemima raced through the door.

"Quick—you must come to the Fourth Form dorm. There's the most terrific storm I've ever seen. I'm sure it's terribly dangerous."

The view from the dormitory window was indeed strange and terrifying. The black clouds had now swept up directly over the school. Yet these were not like English storm clouds, not black lumps moving solidly like angry elephants across the sky. The clouds above Peeg were writhing and boiling as though enormous winds were twisting through them. But there was no noise. After that single grumble of thunder the storm had advanced silently. The hot air hung over the island as heavily as it had the night they had nearly died of thirst.

"The calm before the storm," whispered Jane.

For four minutes this hot calm continued. Then, like a bull breathing out before it charges, a single gust of hot wind swept over them and was gone. They saw the pines down by the burn bend and straighten. A second gust. Stillness again.

And suddenly, with a steady rumbling as thunder trundled from one end of the sky to the other, with a dazzling flicker of lightning, the storm was upon them.

It struck first with a furious blast of wind. The two girls and Mrs. Deal were nearly blown over, but with a great effort they just managed to shut the windows. It grew swiftly dark and they would have seen nothing, except that the lightning flashed so often that it was as bright as a moonlit night. Then with a roar the most tremendous rainstorm crashed onto the school. They heard it rattling on the roof, and windows streamed so much that when they looked out the lightning and the wildly moving trees were bent and distorted.

How long they watched Jane didn't know. Twice pine trees were struck by lightning, flared for a moment, and were then doused when the rain swept furiously over the island again. Sometimes for a few seconds there would be silence and they would think the storm was moving away. Then the wind would roar, and they would hear the answering roar as great waves swept against the little island's cliffs.

Jane was just beginning to think what fun it would be to run out with no clothes on as she had in summer storms at Curl Castle, when she realized something very odd was happening to the window. She could feel, as though a giant's hand was on the other side, the glass pressing harder and harder against her face. Looking up, she saw the catch beginning to give way.

"Quick," she shouted. "The window's opening. Push."

All three of them leaned against the window. But the giant was too strong. For a moment they held it shut, then suddenly, contemptuously, the wind thrust it open, there was a crash as the glass panes smashed against the walls, and Jemima, Jane, and Mrs. Deal were literally blown off their feet by the hurricane that swept in.

Now it was impossible to hear anything but the storm. Jane saw Jemima's mouth moving as she tried to shout something. Bedspreads were lifted off the beds and flung against the walls. But by crawling along the floor and then pulling themselves up by the radiator they were able to look out of the edges of the window again.

They could see the pines thrashing and bending, the burn overflowing its banks, rushing over the lacrosse fields; below them old Macmillan's potting shed had begun to lose its roof, and the large slates were leaping off as though they were tiddlywinks. But it was over the hill, rising from the sea like the giant itself, that they saw what Jane thought was the most terrifying thing she had ever seen in her life. It was a thick black column reaching up into the seething clouds. All round it, darting from its very center, lightning flashed and forked. And as it moved toward them it didn't roar as the wind had done, but howled and screamed like some furious demon determined to kill. A whirlwind—heart of the storm.

Swiftly it moved closer. As it advanced, it bent and swayed.

It could lift a house, thought Jane.

But still they watched. Thunder crashed repeatedly, and sometimes spirals of lightning spun down the black column and flashed into the sea. It was not till Jane saw a clump of large firs snatched effortlessly from the ground that she realized they were in danger. The whirlwind was now moving across the island—and it was heading straight for the school.

"Quick," she shouted to the others. "We must escape."

But her voice was drowned by the shrieking of the wind. And looking at Mrs. Deal and Jemima, Jane thought that even if they had heard they wouldn't have moved. They stared dreamily out into the lightning and watched the whirlwind move toward them with happy smiles. Jane seized their hands and pulled.

Out in the corridor, however, they recovered at once. The school shook and shuddered, its old bricks already beginning to feel the fury of the whirlwind. Leaping over the puddles, they ran toward the kitchen.

"Boiler room," Jane had screamed, but Jemima and Mrs. Deal had already realized that that was their only hope.

In the kitchen, Mrs. Deal paused for an instant to gather an armful of brushes and mops, then they wrenched open the back door.

The courtyard was in chaos, and the wind was so strong that several times they were blown onto their faces.

But it was one of these gusts which saved them. Suddenly, in a heap, they were blown right across the yard and against the boiler room door. Jane pushed it open and they almost fell down the four steps.

The whirlwind must now have been almost upon the school. Its scream was deafening. Yet above it, Jane could hear a rending, crashing noise, and looking up she could see that the tiles of the boiler room were already lifting.

Frantically they began to search, digging with their fingers round the flagstones. A patch of tiles was plucked off one end of the boiler room roof. We're doomed, thought Jane; doomed to a terrible death.

And then the flagstone on which Jemima was kneeling tilted up, tipping her over. A chink of light appeared. The flagstone was pushed back, and the gray head of Captain Thomson rose up through the hole.

The moment he saw them, he beckoned them toward him and dropped out of sight. They ran over and scrambled down one by one. Captain Thomson rose up on Sergeant Cobbin's shoulders again and pulled the heavy flagstone back over the tunnel. Almost as he did so there was a deafening, splintering crash and the boiler room finally broke into pieces and disappeared into the whirling sky.

For a few moments they stood in silence looking at each other. At last Jane said, "We would have been killed."

"How did you guess?" said Jemima.

"We didn't notice for quite a time," said Captain Thomson. "Then Sergeant Cobbin thought he'd take a turn on the beach. He said there was a big storm blowing, so we thought we'd come and have a look."

"Captain," said Mrs. Deal.

"Yes, ma'am?" said Captain Thomson.

But Mrs. Deal could say no more. Suddenly, with a low moan and a clatter of brushes and brooms and mops, she flung up her arms and fainted upon the floor of the tunnel.

"Shock," said Captain Thomson decisively. "Nothing serious, but needs a good rest. Come, Sergeant."

Tenderly, the two old men lifted Mrs. Deal in their arms, and with slow steps they all set off toward the Mess. Jane and Jemima walked at the back carrying the cleaning things.

5

LIFE ON THE ISLAND OF PEEG

Mrs. Deal had almost recovered after a good night's rest, but the two soldiers insisted that she stay in bed, with bundles of old wartime magazines and jugs of hot lemon squash. Jane and Jemima would have been rather bored cooped up in the Mess, but Sergeant Cobbin suggested that this might be a good time for their tour.

The entrance from the beach split almost at once into two forks. If you took the right-hand fork you found yourself on a long sloping ramp which went all round the cavern, gradually rising in spirals to its top. Halfway up the ramp, a round opening showed where the main tunnel began, and three-quarters of the way up was the stout wooden door which led into the Mess. The left-hand fork from the beach entrance led straight to the Mess.

The Mess itself consisted of two corridors with rooms leading off them. You can see how the various rooms fitted by looking at the plan on page 72. The Blowup Room contained the complicated mechanism for blowing up the island. Over the years, however, it had become gradually filled with Captain Thomson's rocks. These had even

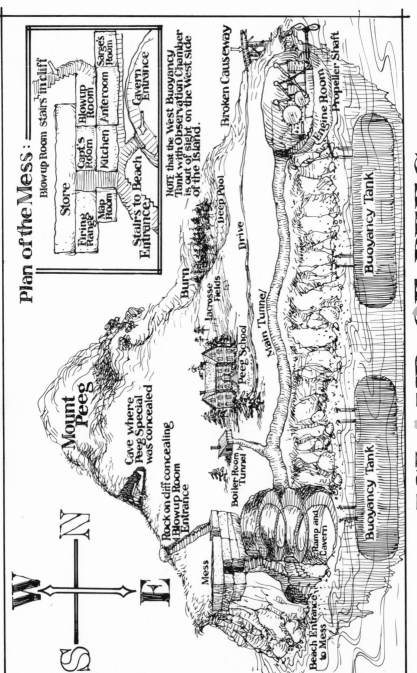

ISLAND OF PEEG

Plan of the Mess:

Blowup Room stairs in cliff

Store
Firing Range
Map Room
Capt's Room
Blowup Room
Kitchen
Anteroom
Sarge's Room
Cavern Entrance

Stairs to Beach Entrance

NOTE that the West Buoyancy Tank with Observation Chamber is out of sight on the West Side of the Island.

Mount Peeg

Cave where Peeg Special was concealed

Rock on cliff concealing Blowup Room Entrance

Burn

Lacrosse Fields

Deep Pool

Broken Causeway

Drive

Peeg School

Main Tunnel

Boiler Room Tunnel

Engine Room

Propeller Shaft

Mess

Ramp and Cavern

Beach Entrance to Mess

Buoyancy Tank

Buoyancy Tank

W N E S

overflowed onto the staircase that led from the Blowup Room to the cliffs. The opening here was concealed among a small outcrop of boulders.

After they had thoroughly explored all the rooms Sergeant Cobbin said it was time to see inside the island. He and Captain Thomson normally used two old bicycles, but he had soon made a box with wheels, just large enough to hold them both, which he could tow behind his bicycle.

After lunch he wheeled this into the tunnel opening and pressed a switch in the wall. They saw that the tunnel sloped steeply down and then bent to the left, so that all they could see was the electric light shining round the corner. They climbed into the box, Sergeant Cobbin swung his leg over the saddle, and they were off.

Although the Island of Peeg was only a mile long and three-quarters of a mile wide, Sergeant Cobbin and Captain Thomson had dug more than twenty miles of tunnels. These crossed and recrossed the island in all directions, none of them straight and all going up and down like country lanes in Wiltshire. As they rode along, Sergeant Cobbin explained that the tunnels twisted because they had had to follow the soft veins of pumice stone running through the rock.

Every twenty yards or so there was an opening in the wall, and after a while, when Sergeant Cobbin stopped to turn off the electric light in one section of the tunnel and turn it on in the next, Jane asked him what these openings were.

"Come with me," said the Sergeant, "I'll show you."

They walked down a short passage, Sergeant Cobbin pushed open a door, turned on the light, and they were in a low square room the size of a bathroom. It was packed from floor to ceiling with wooden boxes on each of which was written EXPLOSIVE—HIGHLY DANGEROUS.

"TNT and dynamite," said Sergeant Cobbin. "The whole island's a bomb. You could do a tidy bit of damage with this island. Or you *could* have done," he added sadly, no doubt remembering again that the war had ended.

"But isn't it very dangerous?" said Jemima. "I thought you could blow up high explosive by sneezing."

"Oh, no—no fear of that," laughed Sergeant Cobbin. "But of course explosive is dangerous stuff. If you could get behind those boxes to the back you'd find the ventilation tunnel. That's a narrow pipe cut through the pumice stone which carries fresh warm air to all the explosive rooms so that they stay dry and at the same temperature. I put a metal vent at the opening to control the flow. Some of the storerooms you can see the pipe, on account it comes out at the open bit between the boxes."

"How wide is it?" said Jane, immediately thinking it would be rather fun to crawl down it.

"I'd say between eleven inches and one and a half feet," said Sergeant Cobbin. "That'd be about it—eleven inches to one and a half feet."

"And do you mean you dug all these tunnels and the little tunnels and put in the electric light all by your-selves?" said Jemima.

"Well, it weren't *all* that difficult," said Sergeant Cobbin modestly. "The pumice is very soft. But then you might think two or three miles of new tunnel every year weren't too much. That's about what we managed. But, as you says, there was the ventilation tunnel to dig, your electrics to put in, your explosives to move; then we lost a lot of time with the Captain going after his rocks and his fossils . . . oh, there was a fair old bit of work, I can tell you. And of course the Captain and I didn't get any younger, as you can imagine."

"I think it's marvelous," said Jemima.

"So do I," said Jane.

"Well, thank you," said Sergeant Cobbin. "Thank you kindly. But you haven't seen the best yet. Now I'll really show you something."

They hurried after him out of the explosive room and climbed into the box again. Before they set off, Sergeant Cobbin said, "I was going to take you to the west buoyancy tank, but I think we'll leave it till another day. There's no knowing how that old iron is standing up to the storm, and we don't want an accident. The buoyancy tanks are frightening enough at the best of times. But make sure you remind me to take you later, and there's the Observation Chamber you must have a run round in."

After half an hour the tunnel came to an end at a wall of gray rock. In the middle of the wall was a door. "Now just wait till you see this," said Sergeant Cobbin. He pushed open the door, turned several light switches, and stood aside.

They were standing on the topmost of about six steel catwalks which went round and across a fairly large, well-lit cavern. Steel ladders and steps ran up and down between the catwalks. And filling the cavern, thrusting spokes and wheels and boilers and pipes and gleaming brass knobs and dials and levers up among the ladders and steps and catwalks, was an immense amount of machinery.

Sergeant Cobbin stood and beamed at it. "Twin cam-shaft interlocking rotary units," he said. "Runs on diesel oil and crude slick same as the *Queen Mary*. Each unit develops eight thousand horsepower, turns the screw at eleven thousand revs a minute. What do you think of her?"

Jane looked. She felt rather disappointed, though quite what she had expected she wasn't sure.

"It's very clean," she said at last.

Jemima, more sensibly, said, "What does that big wheel over there do?"

At once Sergeant Cobbin stumped toward it. "That turns the rotary pump and brings the fuel forward for burning," he said. "Follow me round and I'll run through her with you."

He took them over the whole polished mountain of the engine. He explained each dial and valve, every pipe and every nozzle. In one corner a sort of baby engine, attached to the main one by wires and tubes, was actually running, to supply, Sergeant Cobbin said, dried warm air to the ventilation tunnels and to make electricity.

"How fast can the island go?" said Jemima.

"And why couldn't you just drive us home?" asked Jane.

"Ah, there's the pity of it," said Sergeant Cobbin. "In all the years I tended these engines I never had an opportunity to run them. Then just when my chance came, when I'd had them going a week or two and was getting to know them nicely, they packed it in. Also, that explosion bent the propeller shaft. But I am working on that too. If you'd like to come down I'll explain how it's going."

But the two girls, who were already exhausted with explaining, hastily said thank you, but they really ought to get back to supper or Mrs. Deal would be worried. Sergeant Cobbin was obviously sad to leave his engines, but at the idea of Mrs. Deal getting worried he agreed they must go, and five minutes later they were bumping along the tunnels again.

So began the last happy weeks on the Island of Peeg. Day after day the wind blew them on, veering now east, now west, but on the whole south down the middle of the Atlantic. Captain Thomson, who had once learned navigation, plotted their course with pins on a battered map of the world which hung in the map room. And each week they watched themselves slide farther and farther down it, passing Africa on the right (as you looked at the map) and South America on the left. Jemima once said she smelled spices, but Captain Thomson said she couldn't have because they were six hundred miles from the nearest land.

They went up onto the surface again the day after seeing round the tunnels. The two old soldiers, though they still seemed reluctant to face daylight, went first and said the sea outside was choppy but not rough.

Later, when she and the two girls had climbed up the steep stairs from the Blowup Room which led out onto the top of the cliff, Mrs. Deal stood and faced the sea, breathing deeply.

"How those two good men endured being cooped up for thirty-two years I'll never understand," she said. "My lungs feel like a bag on a vacuum cleaner. I must get on to dusting that Mess directly."

Certainly it was wonderful to be out in the air again. The sky was gray, the wind fresh, but the storm had gone, though it had left many signs of its passage. Shingle, and even quite big rocks, had been flung up from the beach onto the cliff. But it was Jemima who first discovered the most amazing thing the storm had done.

Mrs. Deal and Jane were walking rather slowly, arguing about whether or not to bring school books back so that Mrs. Deal could go on teaching them. "Out of the question," said Jane impertinently, though she could see Mrs. Deal meant it.

Suddenly they heard shouting from the brow of the hill where Jemima had run ahead. She was jumping and shouting and pointing. When they came up to her they saw why.

The school had disappeared. The giant hand of the hurricane had picked it up and put it down—where? Perhaps it was still being carried above the waves and would soon be dumped in Africa, giving someone quite a surprise. But now, in front of them, of those high brick walls, those pointed gables and tall chimneys, not a trace remained.

Or, rather, they found, as they ran (even Mrs. Deal) down the hill toward the school, that there were a few traces. Here some bricks, there a beam of wood or a metal girder accidentally dropped by the hurricane as it had gone screaming and whirling across the island. But even when they were standing exactly where the school had been there was not much more. The boiler room had gone and so had the boiler. The cellars had been scooped out as though by a spoon. Only the bare bricks of the foundations remained.

"What a mercy I remembered the brushes and mops," said Mrs. Deal. "Everything else has gone—the spare polish along with it."

"The compasses too," said Jemima.

"The Land Rover!" cried Mrs. Deal suddenly. "Oh, glory me, I'll never forgive myself—your father's favorite Land Rover."

"Everything," murmured Jane to herself, thinking with pleasure of the school books scattered across the ocean. "*Everything*," she repeated and then, thinking of all the dormitories and the gym mats and the butter pats on the ceiling and Miss Boyle's brogues and the desks and the inkwells and maps and rulers and erasers, all of these gone forever, suddenly Jane felt very gay and began to run about shouting at the top of her voice, "EVERY-THING'S GONE! EVERYTHING'S GONE! EV-ERYTHING'S GONE!"

On the way back to the Mess, Mrs. Deal moaned and lamented the loss of the Land Rover. She interrupted this only once, to say gravely to Jane, "Now, Miss Jane, I meant what I said about lessons. Mr. and Mrs. Charrington would never forgive me if I didn't arrange something."

"You've just been saying they'll never forgive you anyway, so I don't see why you bother," said Jane crossly.

"That will do," said Mrs. Deal. "I shall speak to the Captain about it directly."

By the next day the rough weather had completely disappeared, and once more the sun shone all the time, the warm seas sparkled, and slowly they drifted south, over the equator and on and on and on, feeling, as Jane said, that no human eye had ever gazed on those waters before.

At first Captain Thomson and Sergeant Cobbin refused to go out at all, except in the evening, when they would mooch uneasily about on the beach in the shade of the cliff. But then one day Mrs. Deal said she thought a nice tan was most becoming. Preferably, she said, on a sailor, though actually, she added, she was really getting fonder and fonder of the Army.

This simple remark had an immediate effect on the two soldiers. The very next afternoon Jane discovered Captain Thomson stretched out behind a rock dressed only in his shorts with a flannel over his face. A day or two later, walking along the cliff, Jemima thought she saw a large white bird on the top of Mount Peeg. But climbing carefully toward it, she realized quite quickly that it was Sergeant Cobbin with no clothes on at all.

After thirty-two years away from the sun it was hardly surprising they both got badly sunburned, and Mrs. Deal had to rub tinned margarine all over them.

"You should be ashamed of yourselves," she said. "Two great grown men like you." Sergeant Cobbin and Captain Thomson did look rather ashamed, and after that were more careful. By the end of a fortnight Sergeant Cobbin had turned a lovely golden peach color. Captain Thomson, to his irritation, only went a rusty red and became covered with freckles.

Mrs. Deal led a life which was in fact little different from the one she'd led in Aldeburgh. Every day she marked out some extensive stretch of tunnel and carefully swept it down and dusted it out. She cooked all the meals and explained to Jane and Jemima that, though of course they weren't born when the war was on, they could probably understand what pleasure it gave her to use her old wartime recipes again. The two girls did understand, but they rather wished Mrs. Deal realized that if you hadn't been in the war there was considerably less pleasure in *eating* the old recipes. Pilchards on toast, whale-steak pie, dried-egg scrambled egg, carrot tart—luckily they still managed to catch quite a lot of fresh fish, which made things better.

Mrs. Deal also had to pay quite a lot of attention to the old soldiers. Captain Thomson and Sergeant Cobbin wanted her to inspect everything that they did, probably, Jane thought, because they had been starved of a woman's gentle touch for so long.

"I wonder if I might trouble you for your advice, madam?" Captain Thomson would ask. "I am sure, like most women, you have green fingers."

Sergeant Cobbin built an even larger trailer to fix to the back of his bicycle and would trundle her off to see his engine room, journeys from which he would return red and panting, while Mrs. Deal would say, "Next time, Sergeant, I shall insist you let *me* tow *you*."

"A man's as young as he feels, Mrs. Deal," the Sergeant would gasp.

Despite their age, Mrs. Deal's attention stimulated the

two soldiers to a great deal of work. Captain Thomson rediscovered an interest in gardening. Every morning and evening, to avoid the heat of the day, he would dig Mr. Macmillan's vegetable patch. The hurricane had plucked every plant by the roots, but Captain Thomson found several packets of seeds in the storeroom, and in time the hot sun and frequent watering produced huge lettuces, potatoes, carrots, peas, and tomatoes. He also found flower seeds and before the month was up was arriving with bunches of enormous geraniums, marigolds, and Michaelmas daisies every morning. These he courteously presented to Mrs. Deal with a brisk bow, somewhat to Sergeant Cobbin's irritation.

In the afternoons the Captain arranged his fossils and rocks and wrote out neat cards saying what they were and where he had found them. He also studied his *Encyclopedia of 2000 Famous Painters.*

The interest and praise of Mrs. Deal produced a friendly rivalry between the two soldiers. (Or fairly friendly. Jane sometimes noticed quite a glint in Captain Thomson's eye as he staggered in with another basket of vast new potatoes or a bouquet of gigantic chrysanthemums. And when Sergeant Cobbin asked Mrs. Deal if she'd like to come and see how the propeller shaft was doing, he made sure Captain Thomson was listening.)

Of the two, Jane thought what Sergeant Cobbin did was more interesting. First of all, there was the aeroplane. Sergeant Cobbin produced this from the storeroom a few days after the hurricane. It was contained in seven large crates marked PEEG SPECIAL, and they all helped him drag these up the Blowup Room stairs to the clifftop. Next the plan of the aeroplane was pinned to the side of the largest crate.

"First, Box A," said Sergeant Cobbin, looking at the

plan. Box A contained dozens of six-foot wooden struts and coils of thin, tough wire. The struts had to be joined together by glue and screws to form the framework of the Peeg Special. This took Sergeant Cobbin a week. Next came Box B, which contained the wings. Box C held the wheels and tail.

As he worked, watched by the two girls, and sometimes by a gracious Mrs. Deal, Sergeant Cobbin told them about his life as a boy in Suffolk.

Gradually the plane grew before their eyes, and soon only Boxes F and G remained. Box F contained the engine, and Sergeant Cobbin had to test this before fitting it in. He knocked long steel rods all round it and then tied the engine to them with wire. "That'll keep her from flying away," he said.

All one hot afternoon the island shook to the sound of the bellowing engine. Every so often Sergeant Cobbin stopped it and tinkered with his screwdriver. Eventually, when it was almost impossible to stand behind the propeller for the rush of air, and when you could see the rods straining from the ground, he decided it was perfectly tuned and carefully bolted it into the front of the Peeg Special.

Box G contained the skin of the plane. It also contained various small things like gloves and cushions for the cabin and a tin of paint with which Sergeant Cobbin wrote PEEG on the sides behind the propeller.

The cabin had three seats and a space for luggage, but it was very small. Sergeant Cobbin explained that the Peeg Special had two fuel tanks, which could hold enough to fly about sixteen hundred miles. Top speed was 220 miles per hour, which Sergeant Cobbin thought quite fast. Jane and Jemima hadn't the heart to tell him how much faster planes went now than they had done in the war.

The afternoon it was finished, Sergeant Cobbin said he would try to fly the plane the next day. The two girls spent the morning walking very slowly along the clifftop picking up stones and rocks. Captain Thomson, who had been a trifle standoffish while the plane was being built, now came generously forward to help pull it into line, pump up its tires, and generally assist with all the other little things that were so necessary. Mrs. Deal put the final stitches in a parachute she had been making secretly all this time as a surprise.

After a light lunch, Sergeant Cobbin put on his helmet and goggles. ("Fancy me knowing an airman now!" cried Mrs. Deal.) Then he had a few words with Captain Thomson, shook them all by the hand, and walked slowly over to the Peeg Special, which looked very frail and rickety standing beside the empty boxes. Captain Thomson followed him, and Mrs. Deal and Jane and Jemima hurried a little way up the side of Mount Peeg to get a good view of the flight.

They saw Captain Thomson pour can after can of petrol into the tank, while Sergeant Cobbin fussed about, tightening screws and testing struts. Then the two old soldiers shook hands, talked a moment, shook hands, and suddenly, bending forward, embraced each other. Sergeant Cobbin climbed briskly into the cockpit and pulled his goggles over his eyes. Captain Thomson strode round to the nose and stood with his large hands resting on the propeller.

"Right, sir," they heard Sergeant Cobbin shout.

Captain Thomson raised himself on his toes and with a downward heave pulled on the propeller. It spun down, the engine coughed, the propeller stopped. Again Captain Thomson heaved. Again it spun and coughed, stopped. Captain Thomson put his hands to his back and slowly straightened. He raised his hands for the third time, paused, and this time pulled so hard he stumbled forward and nearly fell.

The engine coughed, coughed again—and with a roar and puffs of smoke the propeller began to spin. Captain Thomson just had time to run out of the way, and the Peeg Special was bumping along the grass. Faster and faster, bump, bump, bump; but not nearly fast enough to take off, Jane thought. It looked as though it might crash over the edge where the cliff fell into the sea. "Please don't let it," Jane whispered. Sparks were coming from the exhaust pipes. And suddenly—it was flying! An extra bump seemed to bounce it into the air, and then it was turning away over the sea and climbing higher and higher into the blue sky.

They all jumped and waved. Even Captain Thomson was leaping about and waving an oily rag in his hand. When Sergeant Cobbin came flying past low over the ground, he took off his goggles and shook them in the air. Three times he circled and then, bumpily but safely, landed on the clifftop.

After that he flew nearly every day, and they all took turns going up in the little cabin. At night they helped him push the Peeg Special into a large shallow cave in the side of Mount Peeg, just in case there was another hurricane. They shut up the mouth of the cave with some old sheep hurdles stuffed with dead heather and bracken. So dry and dead was the whole surface of the island by now that this made the cave mouth look just like a part of the hillside, and it was difficult to recognize even when you were quite close.

The other thing which Sergeant Cobbin worked at was not quite as interesting. This was his engine room, and in particular his mending of the bent propeller shaft. Every afternoon he rode slowly off into the tunnels with tools or, occasionally, with Mrs. Deal in the box behind. Jane and Jemima sometimes went too, more to hear about his life in Suffolk than to watch him work, which was rather boring even though Sergeant Cobbin explained exactly what he was doing all the time.

"Actually," Jane said to Mrs. Deal after one of these visits, "it's *because* of all the explaining that it is boring."

"The Sergeant is a very clever man," said Mrs. Deal. "So, indeed, is the Captain. I've quite come round to the Army."

"So I've noticed," said Jane.

One morning, nearly a month after the hurricane, Sergeant Cobbin said at breakfast that the propeller shaft was now straight.

"She's ready when you are," he said to Captain Thomson.

Captain Thomson made some calculations and eventually said that he thought their best course was to aim for South Africa. Sergeant Cobbin, almost speechless with excitement, started the engine, the Island of Pegg slowly swung round, course was set, and slowly, very slowly they began to move toward the Cape of Good Hope.

So the days passed. Mrs. Deal carried out her promise and made sure they had lessons. But as she was busy keeping the Mess clean, sweeping the tunnels, and cooking the meals, she had to leave the teaching to the two soldiers. On Monday Sergeant Cobbin taught them shooting on the rifle range. On Tuesday he taught them how to fly an aeroplane (not actually flying, but sitting in the cockpit and being taught how to fly). On Wednesday morning they had drill; in the afternoon Captain Thomson taught them art appreciation, which was mostly dates and influences. On Thursday they had, in the morning, platoon tactics (fire and movement) and judging distance; on Thursday afternoon they did the Bren gun, the two-inch mortar, or the hand grenade. Friday was geology. On Wednesday and Thursday lessons took two hours, but the rest of the time they were only an hour, so it wasn't too bad.

Despite much searching from the clifftops, Jemima and Jane never saw any sea monsters. Porpoises they saw, sometimes a great many, rolling past like gray balls, now on top, now underneath the sparkling waves. Also flying fish, which would suddenly skip out of the water and skim across it, occasionally landing on the shingle. The two girls, who had soon discovered they weren't good to eat, would hurry down and throw them back.

Nor did they see a single ship. Nothing stood out on the great flatness which surrounded them. Two or three times they did see aeroplanes, miles up and impossible to hear, pulling the white thread of their vapor trails across the sky. But, as Jane remarked, even though Peeg was a mile long and three-quarters of a mile wide, from that great height it could only have appeared as a speck upon the limitless ocean.

So the days passed—and so no doubt they would have continued to pass for the month or so that Captain Thomson had estimated it would take them to reach Cape Town—when one day something happened which Jane was to remember with terror ever after and which introduced a whole new element of danger into their peaceful and happy lives.

6

HOW JANE AND SERGEANT COBBIN NEARLY DROWN

IT WAS, as usual, a fine day. The Island of Peeg (or the Good Ship Peeg, as Mrs. Deal had taken to calling it since the island had begun to move under its own power again) had been thrusting steadily north for about two weeks, when Jane suddenly remembered the Observation Chamber. It was at breakfast.

"Sergeant Cobbin," Jane said, "do you remember you asked us to remind you to remember to take us to see the Observation Chamber?"

"I do," said Sergeant Cobbin slowly, pouring some condensed milk over his porridge.

"I'm reminding you now," said Jane.

"Well, let me get some breakfast inside of me," said Sergeant Cobbin, "and we'll have a go."

When they had eaten, the two girls helped Mrs. Deal wash up in what she now called the galley. (The two soldiers had at first been quite offended at her nautical terms, and Captain Thomson had even said, "We used to call that the cookhouse, madam." But Mrs. Deal had soon won them round.)

When the galley was shipshape, Sergeant Cobbin wheeled his bicycle down the sloping ramp, the two girls climbed into the box, and they set off.

After twenty minutes and several hundred yards of tunnel, he turned into a narrow tunnel on the left. It seemed to Jane, as they bumped on, that it was getting colder.

All at once the bicycle stopped. Sergeant Cobbin climbed off his saddle. "Here we are," he said. "West buoyancy tank."

They were in front of a small iron door set in the rock. On this, just visible in the dim blue light from a bulb in the roof, was a faded notice: DANGER.

"We'll be about thirty-five feet below sea level here," said Sergeant Cobbin in his slow Suffolk voice. He tapped the walls of the tunnel. "You get a fair amount of seepage."

Jane and Jemima reached out their hands and found that the walls were, in fact, dripping wet.

"Is it quite safe?" Jemima said.

"Oh, you're safe enough *here*," said Sergeant Cobbin. "It's in the buoyancy tank I always feel a bit nervous."

He was standing with his ear pressed to the iron door; now he raised his fist and knocked twice. They heard the door ring with a hollow, empty sound.

"No water behind that, then," said Sergeant Cobbin. "So far so good."

He drew back the bolt and, putting his shoulder to the door, pushed it slowly open. Then he reached inside and turned on a switch.

Jane saw narrow stone steps cut in a thin cleft down through the rock. Another blue bulb shed a feeble light. Sergeant Cobbin walked down the steps and stopped at another iron door at the bottom. Once more he listened, and again raised his fist and brought it down with a heavy thud on the door.

And then they heard one of the strangest sounds they had ever heard in their lives. From behind the door there came, in answer to Sergeant Cobbin's knock, a long, low, echoing note, as though an immense gong had been struck in the depths of a mine. It reverberated and echoed for about half a minute, and during it they heard grow a second sound, a hushed whispering, rushing sound like wind in pines or the sea through a fog.

Twice more Sergeant Cobbin thumped his fist, and twice more the gong echoed and whatever it was hissed and whispered; then he said, "Well, that do sound empty enough. In we go then."

"I don't want to," said Jemima suddenly.

"What's that?" said Sergeant Cobbin.

"I'm frightened," said Jemima tearfully. "Don't let's, Jane."

"Oh, don't you worry," said Sergeant Cobbin in a kind voice. "I've been laying it on a bit. There's nothing to be afraid of. Come on now, Jemima, be a brave girl."

"I think it's dangerous," said Jemima.

"What about you, Jane?" said Sergeant Cobbin, beginning to look rather disappointed.

"I don't know," said Jane slowly. "Well—yes, I think I'll come. But I don't see why Jemima should if she doesn't want to."

"No one must come if they don't want to," said Sergeant Cobbin. "Now, Jemima, my dear, you go and sit comfortably in the box behind my bike. We'll only be gone about twenty minutes, less than that I daresay."

Watching her walk slowly up the steps, Jane suddenly felt that it was really Jemima who was being brave. She had admitted being afraid; but Jane, who was also afraid, wanted to impress Sergeant Cobbin and didn't dare say she was frightened. She almost called out and chased after Jemima, but Sergeant Cobbin had already pushed the second door open and was saying, "Come on, Jane," so she stepped through.

They were standing quarter-way up the inside of what looked like the largest airship in the world. Peering down its dark curving side, Jane could hardly see the bottom below her, despite the lights strung out along the ceiling far above. And it was quite impossible to see the ends. It smelled dank and unpleasant.

"Well, she seems to be holding firm enough," said Sergeant Cobbin, "though there do look to be a bit of water down there at the bottom." His voice was echoed by a hollow booming, followed by the rustling sound, this time much louder.

Sergeant Cobbin said, "This here, the west buoyancy tank, is much the biggest of the tanks, by reason the engineers found this side of the island has a lot of granite." (*Boom, boom* went the buoyancy tank—*booooooooom.*) "It's 100 yards long and 150 feet high. The steel plates are an inch thick, and it be pinnacled to the island every ten yards with five-inch-thick steel bars driven five feet into the rock."

Comforted by his Suffolk voice, Jane began to feel better. "That sounds safe enough," she said.

"Yes," said Sergeant Cobbin. "Oh, they're strong all right. But there's been the explosion that set Peeg off, and there's been the hurry-cane. And don't you forget these tanks have been underwater thirty-two years. That's a long time. Listen." Putting down his foot, he scuffled at the side of the tank. At once there came the slithering, sighing sound Jane had heard before. "Rust," said Sergeant Cobbin. "There's a good quarter inch of it all over the sides, and we don't know how much outside. I wouldn't gladly spend a night in one of these, not when that were rough, that I wouldn't."

"Is it safe to go on now?" said Jane anxiously. "Perhaps we'd better get back to the Mess."

"Well, you wanted to see the Observation Chamber," said Sergeant Cobbin. "She's lasted thirty-odd years, I reckon she'll last another half an hour. We'll get along to the Chamber now. You'll be safe enough there."

Jane found that the side sloped quite gently and was easy to walk down. Each footstep echoed and boomed, sending cascades of rust ahead of it. Quite soon she reached Sergeant Cobbin, who was standing near the bottom looking at a long pool of water.

"Bit more than when I was here last," he said. "Must be a small leak somewhere." He turned left and set off up the tank. "I'll show you the Observation Chamber," he said, "then we'd best be getting back."

Jane hurried after him. Strong as the lights had seemed from the entrance, the top of the tank was so far above them that it was quite gloomy at the bottom. She didn't want to get left behind by Sergeant Cobbin.

After about five minutes of echoing walk, the rust rather like sand under their feet, they reached the end. Here the tank came to a blunt point, about four feet across with a round door, firmly bolted, in its middle. Sergeant Cobbin undid this, to reveal a short tunnel with another round door at its end. He crawled through, opened the farther door, and continued into the Observation Chamber. Then, when Jane followed him, he crawled back, locked both doors, and joined her again.

But Jane noticed none of this. The sight that met her eyes from the Observation Chamber was so wonderful, so extraordinary, that she could think of nothing else.

They were in a round glass bubble held motionless in the middle of the sea. To their left, Jane could see through the clear water the great bulk of the island, the rocky, jagged side of it, stretching forward and backward, up and down—but down only about sixty feet, where suddenly, frighteningly, it ended in jagged points hanging above the immense blue depths of the ocean. Looking down through the glass floor of the Observation Chamber into these depths, at the ragged chunks of rock at the bottom of Peeg, Jane suddenly got the strange feeling that she was standing on her head looking up between her feet at the sky and that the ragged points at the bottom of the island were mountain peaks. Except that, instead of the sky being pale, the blue of the deep water was dark, and the deeper she looked the darker it became until finally her gaze became lost in a deep, dark, blue blackness. It was with relief she looked at the surface. This was about forty feet above them, and she could see the sun sparkling and rippling, broken into dazzling fragments by the waves. But she found that it was actually impossible to see through this surface. There was no sign of the island above the sea; only an endless, shifting, undulating mirror through which, or into which, thousands of lights were shining. Behind the Observation Chamber bulged the west buoyancy tank like a vast rust-colored cigar. Jane could see on her left where it was fastened into the rock by a safe-looking rod.

And everywhere, below, above, on all sides, darting, lazing, sinking, rising, were thousands of fish. Little gold fish twinkling round the glass sides of the Observation Chamber like specks of dust; larger rainbow-colored fish swimming in shoals and diving down into the rocky holes and crevices beneath Peeg; and there were one or two quite big gray fish, which swam steadily and purposefully through the water and then suddenly sped forward and slowed down again for no visible, but obviously for a sensible, reason.

"Well, what do you think of it, eh?" said Sergeant Cobbin.

"It's marvelous," said Jane. "It's the most marvelous, wonderful, extraordinary, marvelous sight I've seen."

"Well, it is interesting," agreed Sergeant Cobbin in a gratified voice. "I don't know why we don't come down more often. Of course, the water wasn't so clear in Scotland. You didn't get quite what you might call such a fishy effect."

"What's that?" said Jane, pointing to a largish drum at the side of the Observation Chamber. A thin cable was wound round it, the end of which disappeared back into the buoyancy tank.

"Well, it's like this," said Sergeant Cobbin. "When you want to go on an Observation trip you pull this lever and that breaks the connection between you and the tank. Then you release the drum and the cable pays out to a distance of a mile and a half. You stay joined to the tank so's you can wind yourself back. Now, you see that little old engine slung underneath us there? That can take her round a bit to see what's going on."

"Can we go on a trip now?" said Jane eagerly. "Let's drive off now."

"Well, not now," said Sergeant Cobbin. "We ain't tried her out for more'n a year. I'll test her out tomorrow and then we'll see."

"Oh, go *on*," said Jane.

"No, miss," said Sergeant Cobbin. "Captain Thomson wouldn't allow it and I agree with him."

One of the large gray fish swam up to the curving side of the Observation Chamber and seemed to be looking in. Jane felt she could have touched it. She felt she was actually in the water itself. And this feeling was even stronger when she looked down. There seemed no reason why she didn't just sink down into the dark blue depths. She pointed down and said, "How deep do you think it is, Sergeant Cobbin?"

"Oh, that'll be several miles," said Sergeant Cobbin. "Terrible pressure down there. If we was to sink we'd be crushed to powder."

"Hardly powder," said Jane. "We'd be too wet. Something more like jam or very flat seaweed." As she spoke, she saw a small rock fall away from the side of Peeg and sink swiftly into the blue. Down, down, down it sank until now she saw it, now she didn't, thought she glimpsed it again, and then it did finally disappear.

"They do say as how even rocks get crushed down there," said Sergeant Cobbin.

"Nonsense," said Jane, but she was impressed all the same.

For twenty-five minutes they stood and watched the marvels of the sea. Then Sergeant Cobbin said they'd best be getting back. He was just about to unbolt the steel porthole which led to the tube into the buoyancy tank when Jane said, "Listen—what's that?"

Sergeant Cobbin cocked his head and listened. "I don't hear nothing," he said after a minute.

"Yes," said Jane. "It's gone now, but I definitely heard it, a sort of thrumming sound. Ssssh. Listen."

They listened, and in a moment they heard it quite clearly, not thrumming so much as throbbing, a *thud*, *thud*, *thud* that gradually grew louder, until the Observation Chamber began to shake and the fish shot off in droves to hide among the rocks.

"It's a boat!" shouted Sergeant Cobbin. "That's the sound of her engines."

"They sound like very big engines," shouted Jane. "Per-

94

haps it's the *Queen Elizabeth*." And indeed the throbbing had now grown into a continuous dull, shuddering roar.

"There she is!" cried Sergeant Cobbin suddenly pointing.

And there she was, coming toward the Observation Chamber directly up the line of the west buoyancy tank and not ten, no, not five feet above it. The noise became deafening. For an instant Jane thought there was going to be a collision. The Observation Chamber, in fact the whole tank, leaped and shuddered. The ship was now right above them, her great, swiftly flowing bulk shutting out the sun. Then Jane saw an explosion of bubbles, felt the Observation Chamber pressed down, glimpsed whirling propellers, and then it was already past and the ship was speeding away, the roar growing fainter. But before she could say anything, the Observation Chamber gave a sudden lurch. Jane looked out toward the side of Peeg and saw what was certainly, she realized, one of the most frightening sights of her life.

The west buoyancy tank had in fact been very much more weakened by the hurricane than Sergeant Cobbin had realized; also, thirty-two years of salt water had eaten deep into the unprotected steel. Some of it was less than one-tenth of an inch thick. The sudden vibration of the boat passing so closely overhead was the final straw. As Jane looked, the long bar which joined their end of the tank to the island suddenly snapped. This threw additional strain on all the other bars along the side of the tank. In a moment they had broken loose too and at once, liberated from its bonds, the huge tank burst to the surface like a whale.

Worse was to follow. Jane and Sergeant Cobbin had only time to see that the Island of Peeg, no longer supported by the west buoyancy tank, was sinking over onto its side, when further disaster struck.

Some of the bars had not broken or been wrenched out of the rock, but had instead pulled great pieces of rusty steel plate out of the side of the tank. Into these gaping holes the seawater rushed. The buoyancy tank began to settle lower and lower until the Observation Chamber was three-quarters underwater again. Suddenly, as the far end of the tank began to sink, the Observation Chamber was lifted into the air, paused there, and then, with the speed of a slowly descending lift, the whole tank and Observation Chamber slid downward and in a moment had disappeared beneath the waves.

When the west buoyancy tank ripped itself loose from the island, the settling of Peeg flung Jemina against the iron door. She guessed immediately what had happened because even through the inch-thick metal, securely bolted, she could hear the muffled sucking and gurgling as the sea poured up the passage and surged against the door.

"Oh, Jane, my darling Jane," whispered Jemima. "Oh, please, God, make them all right." And seizing the light off the front of Sergeant Cobbin's bicycle she set off up the passage. As she walked, trying desperately to remember the way among the dark, winding tunnels, tears poured down her cheeks and fell onto the rocky floor.

At about the same time, Mrs. Deal was busy preparing supper in the galley, helped by Captain Thomson who had just arrived with some huge onions.

"They'll do fine," Mrs. Deal was saying, "if I can get the peel off them without crying my eyes out."

Gallant Captain Thomson was about to peel them himself, when the galley gave the most tremendous lurch and they both staggered sideways into the wall.

"Ahoy there! Ahoy there!" cried Mrs. Deal with surprise. "Where's my sea legs gone to then? It must be gale force nine out there again. Another hurricane, I shouldn't wonder."

Captain Thomson, however, having regained his balance, was looking at the light. "Notice how it hangs," he said. "We've tilted toward the west. Now that can't be heavy seas. We've struck something—yet what? There's not a jot of land on the charts for the next six hundred miles."

"A beasty perhaps?" said Mrs. Deal. "Oh, dear."

"We must investigate at once," said Captain Thomson. "Quick—the Blowup Room stairs."

They hurried through to the Blowup Room and up the stairs to the clifftop. Here two extraordinary sights met their eyes.

Though it was plain they had hit nothing—the sea was as flat and calm and empty as always—it was also plain that the island had tilted. The flat grassy stretch at the top of the cliff was definitely sloping gently downhill. And when they looked down at the beach, it had grown about five feet wider.

After they had looked at this strange sight for a moment, Captain Thomson said slowly, "It can mean only one thing. The west buoyancy tank has either sunk or broken to the surface. Quick, Mrs. Deal, we must hurry to see if the girls and Sergeant Cobbin are all right."

But instead of following him, Mrs. Deal just stood pointing out to sea.

"Look!" she said dramatically. "Look yonder, Captain Thomson. There she blows!"

Startled, Captain Thomson stopped and looked, and for

a moment he too thought that what Mrs. Deal had seen was a whale.

About three hundred yards out from the shore the surface of the water was being violently agitated. Vast bubbles appeared and burst. The waves churned and spouted. Suddenly, from the middle of the disturbance, a vast black hump rose swiftly up and then went on rising, higher and larger and longer.

It was a submarine. But it must have been one of the largest submarines in the world. It was black all over, and its bulging metallic smoothness was interrupted only by the conning tower which stuck out like the turret of a small castle. On top of the conning tower was what looked like a large dome of glass.

They stared at it in amazement, and then Mrs. Deal turned to Captain Thomson and grasped his hand. "It's the Navy," she whispered, trembling. "At last."

Captain Thomson looked at the submarine with a slightly peevish expression on his face.

"It certainly doesn't look like the Navy to me," he said. "No distinguishing marks whatsoever. No fleet marks, no convoy marks, no flotilla, line of battle, or harbor or squadron or station marks what-so-*ever*."

By now several men had appeared under the glass dome and seemed to be scannning the island with telescopes. A long pole also appeared, and, as they watched, a flag was pulled to its top and unfurled in the gentle breeze. It was white with a large red tulip in the middle.

"H.M.S. *Tulip*," said Mrs. Deal.

"No doubt some flag of convenience," said Captain Thomson crossly.

At that moment there came the crackling of a loudspeaker across the water, and a voice boomed, "*Tulip* to

Island. *Tulip* to Island. Identify yourself. Identify yourself."

"Good heavens," cried Captain Thomson. "What am I doing here? The girls and Sergeant Cobbin." He immediately ran off along the cliff, shouting over his shoulder, "They may be floating. Get that ship to send a boat. Must hurry."

"Hullo there," boomed the loudspeaker. "Who are you? Answer please. *Tulip* to Island."

Mrs. Deal cupped her hands round her mouth and shouted as loudly as she could, "Ahoy! H.M.S. *Peeg* here. Ahoy! Come ashore. H.M.S. *Peeg* here."

Then she hurried back along the cliff toward the Mess, thinking, as she afterward admitted, less about Jane and Jemima and Sergeant Cobbin than about the impression she would make on the Royal Navy and how she must spruce up a bit.

There was still a lot of air trapped in the west buoyancy tank, and this meant that at first it sank quite slowly. Jane and Sergeant Cobbin could look up and see the bottom of the island disappearing above them. It was rather like looking down on a very ragged range of miniature mountains from a rising balloon. But all the time, with a sinister gurgling and rumbling, huge footballs of air bubbled out of the buoyancy tank and went wobbling up to the surface. They began to sink faster. The bottom of the island became a blur far above them; suddenly there was an extra explosion of escaping bubbles and then silence. Jane's stomach jumped, and then the tank seemed to settle to its task, plunging swiftly downward into the limitless depths of the sea.

"What shall we do?" said Jane.

"I'm thinking," said Sergeant Cobbin.

Everything had happened so quickly that Jane felt she could think of nothing. She guessed Sergeant Cobbin found the same. Yet, despite the appalling danger they were in, it was almost peaceful. Soon it was pitch dark. The only sign that they were sinking was that it began to grow very cold.

Jane wondered what dying would be like. Suddenly the glass of the Observation Chamber would break. Water would pour in and they would drown, all their past lives passing before them. Or perhaps the pressure would kill them. Would it be very quick, like being smacked flat between a giant's two huge, wet hands? Or very slow, like being wound round by a snake, tighter and tighter, round and round . . .

Round and round! Suddenly Jane realized what they must do. "Quick, Sergeant Cobbin," she cried. "The cable. You must unwind the cable."

"Good girl, Miss," said Sergeant Cobbin. "Me brains was addled."

She felt him brush past her; there was a click as he separated them from the buoyancy tank and then a whirring noise as the cable drum began to spin.

Immediately the Observation Chamber started to shoot up. Jane felt her stomach left behind. So fast did the drum spin that there was a smell of burning oil.

It began to grow lighter and warmer. The sea was now a deep black blue, now swimming-pool blue, now pale and watery. They could see fish again, seeming to swirl down as they sped up, and now, far above them and to the right, Jane could see the long black smudge of the island's underneath, floating there, waiting, as they rushed toward it.

"Come and stand by me," said Sergeant Cobbin.

Jane stood beside him and they watched the spinning drum. It was obvious the cable would end before they reached the surface.

It did so. There was a violent jerk, then they continued to rush upward.

"Cable must have broke," said Sergeant Cobbin. "Shows there's some good comes out of everything rusting away."

"I suppose it means that the tank is more than one and a half miles down," said Jane.

"And still sinking," said Sergeant Cobbin.

Now that it was all over, Jane found that the idea of the giant buoyancy tank plunging down through the inky, freezing sea was terrifying. She was trembling.

The next moment they burst out into the sunlight, and the Observation Chamber began to bob and rock on the waves.

Although it had seemed like hours, the whole thing could scarcely have taken ten minutes. But the Island of Peeg had already moved some way, and they now floated about two hundred yards behind it.

"We won't catch her by swimming," said Sergeant Cobbin, a note of pride for his engines in his voice. "I'll get the motor to work."

It started after four tries, and soon they had climbed out onto the shore. They noticed at once that the island had tilted about four feet over to the old west side. "You can see the angle by that green line along the causeway," said Sergeant Cobbin.

Jane and Sergeant Cobbin then set off for the Mess. When they reached the place where the school had been Jane said, "Let's go by the boiler room tunnel, Sergeant Cobbin. It'll feel so safe underground." She still found it hard to realize they were all right again; at the same time, so quickly had everything happened, it was difficult to realize they had been in any danger at all.

They were walking back along the tunnel when all at once Sergeant Cobbin switched off the lights in the section they were in and whispered, "Hush, miss. Listen a moment."

In a moment Jane heard a noise she knew well, a quiet crying, with a little catch and hiccup at the end of each cry—Jemima's crying. At the same time they saw coming up the tunnel from their left the faint wavery beam of Sergeant Cobbin's torch.

"It's Jemima!" shouted Jane. "Turn on the lights. Jemima! Jemima! Where are you?"

There was Jemima, standing amazed in the light of the tunnel. When she saw them she rushed forward and flung herself into Jane's arms.

"I thought you'd drowned," she cried. "I heard those engines and then the sea and—oh, Sergeant Cobbin, Jane, I'm so pleased to see you. Oh, oh, oh." And once again Jemima burst into tears, but this time tears of joy.

At the Mess they found considerable confusion. Mrs. Deal had changed into her best clothes—tweed coat with long tartan scarf, a two-piece jersey wool dress, petal hat, and leather boots. Though smart, these must have been extremely hot. Nevertheless, Mrs. Deal was engaged in a major dusting.

"Now, girls, now, Sergeant Cobbin," she said the moment she saw them, "there's not an instant to lose. Into your best clothes, and then help me get this place ship-shape and Bristol fashion."

"We've had the most terrible time," said Jane dramatically.

"They've been saved from a watery grave," said Jemima.

"No doubt you have," said Mrs. Deal, whirling her duster over the anteroom notice board. "Now out of those clothes and into something respectable. And it's your blues for you, Sergeant. We're hosts to the Senior Service."

"But you don't understand," said Jane. "We're lucky to be alive."

"We're *all* lucky to be alive," said Mrs. Deal. "Or unlucky, depending on how you look at it."

"The lass is right," said Sergeant Cobbin. "We had a narrow squeak right enough, and it were her that saved us."

"See—it's true," said Jane. "It was like this. I'll explain." And before Mrs. Deal could interrupt again she described everything that had happened as fast as she could but without leaving anything out.

Mrs. Deal, though of course she listened, appeared no more than mildly interested. She continued to dust and tidy feverishly, and Jane had to follow her about as she rushed from room to room. When Jane finished with ". . . and so here we are," Mrs. Deal said, still dusting, "Well, that certainly does sound very foolhardy. Very sensible of Miss Jemima not to venture into such a dangerous object.

"But now," went on Mrs. Deal, "I've something really exciting to tell you." She stopped dusting and, after calling Sergeant Cobbin and Jemima in to listen, said in a ringing voice, "The Navy has at last arrived!"

"Where? What? When?" cried Jane and Jemima and Sergeant Cobbin together.

"Yes, the Royal Navy," said Mrs. Deal again. "One of Her Majesty's Warships of the Submarine Class is at present stationed just below the cliff—H.M.S. *Tulip*. I have extended an invitation to the crew to come aboard, though I'm not sure whether they heard me. No doubt, however, they will be sending a landing party. That is why we must clear decks at once. Duster and brooms are in the galley."

But the two girls and Sergeant Cobbin were already running for the Blowup Room stairs and the clifftop.

There, as Mrs. Deal had said, floated the giant submarine. At last they had been discovered. This meant, Jane thought, that they would be rescued. Suddenly she felt rather sad.

Sergeant Cobbin, who may have been feeling the same, was looking very suspicious. "I don't like it," he was muttering. "No proper markings, and that be far too big for a submarine in my opinion. You say the war is over. But who else don't know it? That great thing could lie about not knowing it for a devil of a time. Must have been the thing that passed over the west buoyancy tank and sank her. I wondered why she were so low above us. May have been on purpose."

But Sergeant Cobbin's speculations were cut short by Jemima. "Look," she said suddenly, "there's Captain Thomson. Something's happened."

Coming along the cliff was a sad sight. Head bowed, feet dragging, Captain Thomson was slowly returning to the Mess. Every now and then he stopped and clasped his head in his hands or brushed them across his eyes.

"I know what it is," said Jemima. "He thinks you're dead."

"So he do," said Sergeant Cobbin. "Poor fellow. We'll put him out of his misery." He cupped his hands and shouted, "Captain Thomson. Captain Thomson, sir. We're safe and sound."

But Captain Thomson didn't hear him. He continued to

drag his way slowly and miserably along the cliff, head bowed.

So Jane and Jemima ran toward him, shouting. And suddenly he did hear. He stopped in amazement, looked up, and then flung his arms wide and ran toward them. He picked the two girls up and whirled them round. "Safe!" he cried. "Safe!" But when Sergeant Cobbin came hurrying up, Captain Thomson could no longer contain himself, and Jane saw tears pouring down his cheeks as he seized his old friend in his big arms. All he could say was, "I thought you'd gone, Sergeant. I thought you'd gone."

After a while he felt better and, looking at them all, he said, "But what happened? What in the blazes happened? I saw the tank had gone. You can see for yourself the island's tilted. I thought you'd be at the bottom of the sea."

Now Sergeant Cobbin and Jane had a really interested listener. Indeed, so interested did they all get—with Sergeant Cobbin explaining about Jane's brilliant idea and Captain Thomson saying, "Good gracious and what happened then?" and praising Jemima for her good sense— that none of them noticed that a large boat, laden with sailors, had set off from the submarine *Tulip* and was speeding toward the shore.

7

MR. TULIP

THE FIRST SIGN they had that there were visitors ashore was a voice booming through a loudspeaker from the beach.

"*Parlez-vous Français?*" it boomed. "*Sprechen sie Deutsch? Parlare Italiano?* Do you speak English? *Habla usted Español?* . . .*"

It went on for some time, speaking languages which none of them had ever heard before.

But even odder than all the languages was the effect it had on the two soldiers. With a cry of "Cover!" Captain Thomson flung himself onto his stomach and began to crawl rapidly toward the Mess, with Sergeant Cobbin close behind.

"They're mad," said Jemima. "They think they're Germans who don't know the war has ended."

"I know," said Jane. "Isn't it pathetic?" To the two soldiers she shouted, "They are friends.

"Come on, Jemima," she went on, "let's wave."

The two girls walked to the edge of the cliff and waved down to the fifteen or twenty men on the beach. Several of them waved back.

"They're waving to us," shouted Jemima.

Captain Thomson and Sergeant Cobbin stopped crawling and turned their heads as though listening. Jane wondered if they expected to hear gunfire. After a moment they stood up and came toward the girls.

"You can't be too careful," said Captain Thomson as he came up. "We may *not* be in a time of war, or then again we may." He stared belligerently down at the beach. "Come, Sergeant. We're outnumbered and outgunned. We must parley. Stay here, girls, and keep your heads down."

The two girls, however, followed the soldiers down the cliff path and hid behind one of the large rocks that littered the beach. They saw Captain Thomson and Sergeant Cobbin march grimly up to the men, halt, salute, and then heard Captain Thomson speak in a clipped, official voice.

"May I ask who you are, sir, and by what right you land on the Island of Peeg?"

"I am Commander Hautboyes," said the tall man with the loudspeaker in a slight accent. "I am of the vessel *Tulip*. And you, sir?"

"Captain Thomson of the Seventh Hussars, Sergeant Cobbin of the Seventh Hussars," said Captain Thomson. "Commanding Operation—that is, the Island of Peeg. What do you want? Water? Fresh fruit? What's your business in these waters?"

Commander Hautboyes did not answer at once, and Jane noticed a small white earplug in his ear to which he seemed to be listening. Like all the other men, he was dressed in a spotless white uniform with a peaked hat. The only difference was that he had four red tulips stitched onto his cuffs, whereas his men had only one.

After a pause, Commander Hautboyes said, "I am instructed to invite you to dinner tonight. My Captain would be delighted if you would condescend to honor his table at eight o'clock this evening."

"Well, I don't know," said Captain Thomson slowly. "I'd like to know a bit about you. What flag do you sail under? I know the war is apparently and officially over, but I daresay, well—y'know, pockets of resistance and so on; what I'm driving at, to speak plainly, is—are your intentions peaceable?"

"One moment, *mon capitaine*." Commander Hautboyes spoke rapidly into the mouthpiece of the loudspeaker, but, as no noise came out, he must have flicked some switch which put him in touch with the submarine. Once more he listened intently, holding the small white earplug with his hand.

At last he said, "*Mon capitaine*, I am instructed to tell you that all your questions will be answered this evening. But may I assure you that our intentions are entirely peaceable. A boat will be here at eight o'clock less ten minutes."

Captain Thomson and Sergeant Cobbin saluted. Commander Hautboyes shouted a few orders, the sailors climbed into the boat, and soon they were chugging back to the looming bulk of the submarine.

"We had no choice," said Captain Thomson. "Superior force. Come, Sergeant, we must adjourn to the Mess and discuss tactics. We have only two hours to prepare a plan of action." They at once set off for the Mess, talking earnestly. Jane and Jemima followed behind more slowly, eagerly discussing what the dinner would be like and how exciting it was to be going to see a submarine.

At first, however, it looked as though no one but the two soldiers would go. Despite the two children's desperate entreaties and Mrs. Deal's refusal even to consider not going, Captain Thomson was firm.

However, it was Sergeant Cobbin who changed his mind. Reading, in preparation for the dinner, through a manual on infantry tactics, he came upon a section called "When Dealing with Superior Force." This said that the most important single rule was never to divide your forces. When this was pointed out to him, Captain Thomson immediately saw its sense.

"Hadn't occurred to me," he said. "But of course the Manual's right, as always. While we were at dinner Commander Hautboyes or some other of those fellows could sneak in and take you all. No—we stick together. Get dressed, girls—no time to lose."

Captain Thomson and Sergeant Cobbin's best uniforms had only been worn on Christmas days for thirty-two years. Fortunately they had been well surrounded by mothballs, and Mrs. Deal said that, though they would both smell strongly, they would look smart enough.

"You two girls are the problem," she said, turning to them next. "No doubt the Captain of H.M.S. *Tulip* will be an Admiral at the least. We certainly can't have you both dining at the table of a belted Admiral in jeans and shirts."

Fortunately, Mrs. Deal was a quick worker with a needle. After some thought, she took two of Captain Thomson's summer shirts, rapidly cut and stitched them to fit the girls like short party dresses, and then cut some strips from a length of green mosquito net and sewed them to the cuffs.

They had only just finished dressing when Captain Thomson clanked impatiently into the anteroom and said it was already eight o'clock and they must get down to the beach. He and Sergeant Cobbin were in thick blue uniforms with huge metal epaulets and spurs at their ankles. The weather was still very hot, and Jane felt the men must both have been boiling; as, indeed, was Mrs. Deal who, after taking off her coat and long tartan scarf, had now put them on again, together with her close-fitting hat of brightly colored felt petals.

"Forward," said Captain Thomson. "We are outnumbered and outarmed. But we are British. We shall take no weapons except my ceremonial sword. Guile and cunning shall be our watchwords. Sergeant—the Manual."

"How you do go on, Captain," said Mrs. Deal. "As though we'd anything to fear from our Good Ship *Tulip* of Her Majesty's Royal Navy."

They hurried down to the beach and then crunched along the narrow strip of shingle toward a boat already bobbing close to the shore. Sergeant Cobbin's and Captain Thomson's spurs jingled and clinked loudly on the stones.

It was a smaller boat than before with room for about six in comfortable seats at the back. Commander Hautboyes stood politely waiting for them as they came up.

When he saw Mrs. Deal and the girls he bowed toward them. "I had no idea . . ." he said. "*Les demoiselles* . . ."

"Allow me," said Captain Thomson. "Mrs. Deal—Commander Hautboyes. Miss Jemima Garing, Miss Jane Charrington—Commander Hautboyes."

"*Enchanté, enchanté,*" said Commander Hautboyes, bowing to each in turn. "*Enchanté.*"

A few moments later, having climbed or been helped aboard, they were roaring out over the calm sea toward the still bulk of the submarine.

"I could do with this breeze, sir," said Sergeant Cobbin, holding his hot red face into the wind.

"What?" shouted Captain Thomson.

"I said, 'I could do with this breeze, sir,' " shouted

Sergeant Cobbin. But Captain Thomson shook his head to show he couldn't hear. Mrs. Deal sat bolt upright with her eyes shut.

The boat swung round in a fast small circle and then came gently to rest against the high bulging side of the submarine.

A little above them, one of the steel plates had slid silently open, and a platform moved out above the motor boat. Two sailors hurried out, secured the boat, and lowered some steps.

It took several minutes to get them all aboard. Jane and Jemima skipped up easily enough and so did Sergeant Cobbin, only more slowly. But Captain Thomson kept on getting his sword caught in his legs or the steps and eventually had to hold it out behind him like a tail. Mrs. Deal was still affected by the buffetings of the journey. Keeping her eyes shut, she more or less abandoned herself to the strong arms of the Navy and was almost carried up. Once inside, however, she soon recovered and they all set off after Commander Hautboyes.

At first sight, the submarine seemed rather boring. It seemed to be all steel corridors with a few doors and iron ladders leading off them. There was a low humming all the time, a great many pipes, and every now and then they would pass one of the white-suited sailors, who would salute Commander Hautboyes.

Mrs. Deal, walking close behind the Commander, would graciously incline her head each time this happened. After a while they came to a lift. This carried them swiftly down until they must have been nearly at the bottom of the submarine.

"*Madame, demoiselles, messieurs*—the stateroom," said Commander Hautboyes.

The lift doors opened. They stepped out. The doors

closed behind them, shutting Commander Hautboyes from view.

They were standing in a room which was so grand that for a mad moment Jane thought they had been magically carried to Buckingham Palace. The walls were lined with elegant white panels and hung with huge mirrors and pictures with little lights above them. On the floor was a thick white carpet decorated with scarlet tulips, and scattered upon this were sofas and chairs, a harpsichord, and tables covered with china objects and large expensive-looking books. Opposite the lift wall there were four huge windows with long scarlet curtains. The doors of the lift itself were so cunningly disguised to resemble panels that they were quite difficult to find. Round the room, in huge vases, there were dozens of sweet-smelling bright red tulips.

"Well, I never," said Mrs. Deal.

"No expense spared here," said Sergeant Cobbin, treading the thick carpet appreciatively.

Captain Thomson, whose expression, at the sight of the pictures in their curly golden frames, had become sharp and knowledgeable, now clanked up to one of them and, pretending not to read the large gold label underneath it, said, "Good lord—a Zoffany. Born 1734. Studied in Italy. Influenced by Hogarth. Died 1810. And what's this?" He moved on to the next picture and, after a quick downward glance, said, "Let me see—I'd say a Fragonard. Am I right? Yes. Jean Honoré Fragonard. Goodness me, a Fragonard in a submarine. Born 1732. Studied under F. Boucher and also C. Van Loo. Influenced by Tiepolo. Died 1806. This is the most extraordinary submarine I've ever seen."

"Didn't know as how you'd ever seen a submarine," said Sergeant Cobbin.

"What I meant, Sergeant," said Captain Thomson, "is that if I had I imagine this *would* have been the most extraordinary of them all."

"Oh, I don't agree," said Mrs. Deal. "It's no more than what you'd expect from the Navy. They've always done the best by their men. My husband used to say, 'When the Navy says welfare, they *mean* welfare!' "

"If you'll pardon me, Mrs. Deal," Captain Thomson said stiffly, "welfare is one thing; this—this—well, I can find no words to describe it. This magnificence—extravagance—is something quite different."

"Do you think so?" said Mrs. Deal, taking one of the huge scarlet curtain tassels in her hand. "It's no more than what I'd expect in the Lord High Admiral's quarters."

It looked for a moment as if an argument might start. But at that moment there came the sound of a door opening and shutting from just beside them and a voice cried:

"How perfectly delightful. Cavalry. Gentlemen—welcome to the *Tulip.*"

Standing in the door they saw a short, fat man with carefully brushed, but rather thin, fair hair. He was wearing a white uniform with little red tulips embroidered neatly all over it. He had a fat white face and fat red lips, and as he came closer Jane saw that he was really quite old—about forty.

"My dear friends," he said, "*so* rude of me. The sight of that familiar uniform quite drove the formalities out of my silly head. Let me introduce myself—Mr. Tulip."

He held his hand out, but before anyone could answer, Mrs. Deal, already secretly worried by the white uniforms, burst out, "*Mister* Tulip? Did you say *Mister* Tulip? Do you mean—er, I mean excuse me, sir—but aren't you an Admiral? Are you not an officer in Her Majesty's Navy?"

Mr. Tulip looked at her in astonishment, then suddenly screamed with laughter.

"Alas no, madame," he said at last when he had recovered. "A charming idea. One day perhaps—as a midshipman. But at the moment I cultivate my garden."

"Your garden?" said Mrs. Deal, looking wilder and wilder. "Which garden?"

"An expression, dear," said Mr. Tulip. "Now let us become acquainted."

At this, Captain Thomson made a great hurrumping noise in his throat and introduced them. His face was rather red and hot, and he seemed embarrassed by Mr. Tulip. However, he relaxed a bit when Mr. Tulip said, "Seventh Hussars and—don't tell me, Captain—Third Regiment. What a regiment! What a record! What men!"

"You know them, sir?" cried Captain Thomson eagerly. "Hear that, Sergeant. We—myself and Sergeant Cobbin— would be most interested to hear any news . . ."

"Intimately," said Mr. Tulip. "But let's tell each other everything over dinner. For the moment we'll ask one of my lively lads to get us all a drink."

He walked over to the wall and lightly pulled a long crimson cord. Almost at once, one of the panels in the wall swung open and a large, red-faced young sailor stepped through.

"Now, Mrs. Deal," said Mr. Tulip, "what would you like?"

Mrs. Deal, who was still trying to get over the shock of discovering that Mr. Tulip wasn't an Admiral in the Navy, made a little speech she had plainly prepared before. "I should be proud, sir," she said, "to partake of some grog."

"And Miss Garing and Miss Charrington? What would you like?" Jane and Jemima had Coca-Cola; the two soldiers had whisky. Mr. Tulip said he'd have mineral water with a slice of lemon in it. The young sailor saluted and left the room.

Mr. Tulip turned to Jane. "What do you think of my little place?" he said.

"I'd hardly call it little," said Jane, who found Mr. Tulip rather surprising. "I think it's huge and very grand."

"What I would venture to ask, sir," said Sergeant Cobbin, who was almost bursting with admiration, "what is the exact size of your craft, sir?"

"Fourteen thousand three hundred and twenty tons, six hundred feet long, seventy feet deep, forty-five-foot beam," said Mr. Tulip briskly. "Now—let's have dinner."

As they followed him Captain Thomson said, "Fine collection of pictures, Mr. Tulip."

"Thank you, my dear," said Mr. Tulip.

"I thought I noticed a fine Guardi," said Captain Thomson. "Born 1714, studied under his father Domenico Guardi, died 1793."

"1712, dear," said Mr. Tulip.

"Also studied under Canaletto," intoned Captain Thomson. Then he said, "I beg your pardon?"

"1712," said Mr. Tulip. "Guardi was born in 1712, not 1714."

"1714," said Captain Thomson stiffly.

"Oh, no, definitely 1712," said Mr. Tulip, seeming to lose interest.

Captain Thomson stopped and went very red. "1714," he said loudly.

Mr. Tulip looked at him and then gave a light laugh. "As you will, Captain," he said, "as you will. Mrs. Deal, you lead."

This moment of embarrassment was quickly smoothed

over by Mr. Tulip himself. He spent the first twenty minutes talking entirely about the Seventh Hussars. He found several officers whom he and Captain Thomson both knew, and the old soldier's eyes almost filled with tears as he heard about friends he had not seen for thirty-two years. Mr. Tulip seemed to know nearly as many, if not more, Hussars who were sergeants, corporals, and even privates, and so was able to give Sergeant Cobbin a lot of news as well.

The dining room was as grand as the stateroom. It was paneled in long ornamental mirrors, with occasionally a marble statue in an alcove. Twisted silver candlesticks had tall candles burning in them. When everyone had finished their soup and a delicious *mousse* of hot salmon and they were well into large helpings of tender beef and Yorkshire pudding, which made them all realize how tired they had been getting of fish and wartime tins, Mr. Tulip said, "Now, I'm sure we are all simply dying to know all about each other. You must wonder how I have this submarine; I am certainly very intrigued by the way your charming little island moves through the water at nearly two knots an hour against the current. But let me tell you my tale first. It is a humble story, quickly and simply told."

Humble it certainly was not, though Jane agreed that Mr. Tulip told it quickly enough. He had been brought up and educated in England, and had always had a deep love of the sea (here Mrs. Deal, who had drunk several large goblets of various colored wines and begun to look very sleepy, gave a loud, sympathetic sigh). Unfortunately, his father had compelled him to earn his living in the family nickel mines in Australia. Just after his father had died, gold and oil had been discovered in the mines, and he had been able to retire at a young age with two hundred million pounds. Since then he had sailed the oceans in his submarine, doing good wherever he was able and providing a home for sea-loving youngsters of every nationality, race, and color.

"And there you are," he finished, spreading his podgy hands, "a poor tale, but my own."

"Two hundred million is a fair whack," observed Sergeant Cobbin, no doubt emboldened by the wine. "You'd do better to call it a rich tale but your own."

Mr. Tulip laughed. "A hit, Sergeant, a palpable hit. Poor in incident, almost a dull life, is what I meant."

"Why do all the sailors carry guns?" said Jane.

For a moment Mr. Tulip looked at her without saying anything. Jane felt he was irritated by her. Then he smiled and shrugged his shoulders, "Well, darling, you know how it is. The world's not always a very nice place, and, suddenly popping up as we do out of the sea, we *have* found ourselves in some rather ticklish spots. And then, as the good Captain will tell you, dear, there's nothing like a little arms drill and weapon training to make a youngster brisk and lively."

"They didn't seem all that young to me," said Jane. "Some were proper old men."

"Everyone benefits from arms drill and weapon training, dear," said Mr. Tulip shortly.

Feeling he really was rather irritated, Jane didn't go on, and after a moment, all chins and smiles again, Mr. Tulip begged Captain Thomson to tell him about the island.

Captain Thomson cleared his throat and finished his glass of brandy. Mr. Tulip politely filled it for him again.

"Well," said Captain Thomson, "there's no point in beating about the bush. You'd find out for yourself soon enough, and if, as I understand, the war is now finally over—and I take it this is so, is it, sir?" He looked inquiringly at Mr. Tulip.

"The war?" said Mr. Tulip.

"The 1939 war," said Sergeant Cobbin.

"Yes, my dear," said Mr. Tulip, looking mystified.

"In that case, Operation Peeg need no longer remain a National Secret," said Captain Thomson.

Then he told Mr. Tulip the whole story. As he said later, not only could Mr. Tulip have found it out, or the most important part, which was the explosive, himself, but he felt he could trust a man who had obviously been on close and friendly terms with the Seventh Hussars.

Mr. Tulip was an excellent listener. He looked steadily at Captain Thomson all the time, occasionally lifting his hands in silent admiration or amazement. Only once did he interrupt, and that was when Captain Thomson was describing the amount of explosive packed into Peeg.

"Eight million tons!" he'd cried. "Are you sure? Why, that's more powerful than an atomic bomb. It approaches a hydrogen bomb."

"The figure is quite correct," said Captain Thomson. "No question about that. We checked the entire complement every three months. I signed it over to Sergeant Cobbin one quarter; he'd sign it back to me the next. Helped to pass the time."

At the end of Captain Thomson's account, which took about half an hour and during which Mrs. Deal fell into a deep and rather obvious sleep, Mr. Tulip raised his hands, looked round at them all, and said, "My dears—I'm simply stunned. Such courage! Such resource! And you, Captain, and you, Sergeant—steadfast at your post these thirty-two years. And the adventures since! To think I might have inadvertently caused the destruction of Jane and the good Sergeant here. This is the raw meat of life. You make me feel a schoolboy."

"Come, sir, come, Tulip," said Captain Thomson

gruffly and modestly, his face red. "Only a soldier's duty. A soldier stands by his post, that's all."

"Well, I think it's *heroic*. Really I do," said Mr. Tulip. Then, leaning forward, he said in a serious voice, "But tell me, Captain. Isn't it possible that all that explosive might have—er, gone bad in some way over the years? Got wet or damp or damaged, not be able to explode?"

"Not a chance of that, Mr. Tulip, sir," said Sergeant Cobbin, lolling comfortably back in his chair. "We've a foolproof ventilation and drying system, running on a subsidiary turbine." Briefly, though in full detail, he outlined the system of pipes and vents. Mr. Tulip was soon convinced.

"Fancy," he said, "a hydrogen bomb not three hundred yards away from us. Extraordinary."

They talked a little more about this and that, and then Mr. Tulip suggested they stay the night with him. "Mrs. Deal has had a busy day, as one can see," he said. "I have some comfortable guest rooms. Pray stay."

They all agreed, particularly Jane and Sergeant Cobbin, who had been exhausted by their plunge in the Observation Chamber, which had happened only that morning, though it seemed like days ago.

Indeed, Jane and Jemima were so tired that when they were shown into the room they were to share, they didn't even bother to wash, but just undressed and got straight into bed without any clothes on. They both fell asleep almost at once.

They were awakened at nine-thirty by a small wizened Chinese wheeling in a trolley with two trays of breakfast.

They each had cornflakes and cream, a dainty rose-pat-

terned teapot, a jug of milk, toast and butter and marma-
lade, and two boiled eggs.

"Gosh, aren't the boiled eggs wonderful," said Jemima.

"And the butter!" said Jane. "It's completely fresh."

"What do you think of Mr. Tulip?" said Jemima.

"I think he's rather nice," said Jane slowly. "He's rather
like an actor Mummy and Daddy know who used to come
and stay at Curl Castle. He called everyone darling or dear
too."

Chattering away through breakfast and while they
shared a bath (the water was hot and salty, but the shower
had a notice saying FRESH WATER), they agreed that Mr.
Tulip was nice, but that there was something a bit sinister
about the submarine.

"He was definitely cross when I asked him about the
guns," said Jane.

"Yes, and I think Captain Thomson suspects him of
something," said Jemima.

"I think Captain Thomson is just embarrassed to be
called my dear," said Jane. "He's frightened of emotion."

When they were dressed, the Chinese steward
appeared and politely took them to the stateroom. The
others were already there.

"Ah, my dear Miss Charrington, my dear Miss Garing." Mr. Tulip came toward them with open arms. He
was wearing lavender-colored shorts and a wide straw hat.
"I have asked some of the boys in the galley to prepare us
a little picnic. A *fête champêtre.*"

He led them to a different door and, having shown
them through into a new, rather wide corridor, said,
"Now this is another little device I'm rather proud of. A
moving corridor. Don't be alarmed."

He raised his foot and lightly tapped a small knob on

the floor. Immediately they began to move—and quite fast. Jane and Jemima seized each other, and Captain Thomson's sword, sticking awkwardly against the wall, made a fearful rattling until he hastily pulled it away.

"Oops! Oops!" cried Mrs. Deal.

"Steady, darling," said Mr. Tulip, and gripped her arm.

After a few moments of swift progress the corridor as abruptly slowed and then stopped. They were below five steps leading up to the bridge.

This was about thirty feet long, rather pointed at one end and broader at the other. At the pointed end were a lot of instruments—a spoked wheel, binnacles, rows of levers and dials; in front of these were two large comfortable leather chairs. At the broad end there was an awning, with deck chairs and tables.

The bridge was in an empty steel chamber the same shape as itself and somewhere, Jane supposed, at the bottom of the submarine. When they were all aboard, Mr. Tulip hurried over to the instruments and pulled several levers. Immediately they saw the roof of the chamber slide swiftly back, and at the same time the whole bridge shot upward. A moment later it reached the top of the submarine and they burst out into the sunshine.

They were high above the sea, about forty feet up; in front and behind stretched the submarine.

It was so surprising that for a moment no one could speak. Then Jemima, who had been looking anxiously about, said, "But, Mr. Tulip, where's Peeg?"

Only then did Jane realize that the sea around them was completely empty, and she wondered, for a cold moment of fear, whether Mr. Tulip was as kind as he seemed, and whether perhaps he hadn't carried them away during the night.

But Mr. Tulip laughed kindly and, putting his arm

round Jemima, led her over to a screen among his instruments. Pressing a switch, he lit up a band of light sweeping across it which revealed various bright blobs.

"There's Peeg, dear," he said, pointing to the largest of these. "Fifteen miles away. The good Sergeant's engines haven't faltered."

Though it was nice to be in the fresh air, it was very hot. There was no wind and the sun beat down from almost overhead. Mrs. Deal, whose jersey dress had been comfortable enough in the air-conditioned submarine, began to look very hot. So, indeed, did the two soldiers. They all three now hurried under the awning and fell panting into the deck chairs.

"Don't worry, my dears," called Mr. Tulip. "It will be better when we start." He pulled some more levers, and gradually the huge ship (somehow it seemed too big to be called a submarine) began to glide forward.

Soon they were moving quite fast, with the water churning and whirling far out at the back. Captain Thomson went and stood by the rail and looked over the edge. Mrs. Deal spread in the breeze and abandoned herself to its blowing. Sergeant Cobbin came and joined the two girls beside Mr. Tulip.

"They didn't have nuclear power in your day, Sergeant," Mr. Tulip shouted.

"What's that?" called Sergeant Cobbin.

Jane went over and stood by Captain Thomson, and together they watched the sea split aside as the submarine sped through it.

"Must be doing twenty-five knots," cried Captain Thomson.

"What are knots?" shouted Jane.

"It's how you measure how fast you are going at sea," Captain Thomson shouted back. Jane nodded sensibly and looked down at the rushing, green, foam-covered water, and quite soon, after half an hour, they were rapidly overtaking Peeg.

They arrived at the beach where the Mess entrance was at eleven-thirty. Mr. Tulip lowered the bridge down into the submarine until they were level with the sea. A panel slid open in the side of the submarine; a short walk, and they stepped out into a motor launch. Two sailors came with them to carry one of the picnic hampers.

Mr. Tulip was very excited by the Mess. He rushed from room to room, peering at the faded notices on the notice board and running his fat fingers delightedly over the covers in the anteroom.

"But this is a little *gem*," he kept calling to a rather embarrassed Captain Thomson. "A jewel. It's authentic to the last *detail* And so *comfortable*, Captain. And don't I detect"—Mr. Tulip turned a roguish eye on Mrs. Deal, at the same time indicating a vase of wilting flowers—"a woman's gentle hand? How they must have relished your soothing presence, dear, after those harsh years alone."

"Indeed we did," said Sergeant Cobbin. "A right change she made and no mistake."

Mrs. Deal tut-tutted modestly and went off to change out of her jersey dress. Mr. Tulip now asked if he could be shown the tunnels, and the three men set off.

One thing had rather surprised Jane and Jemima. When Captain Thomson had shown Mr. Tulip round the Mess he had carefully avoided the Blowup Room. Mr. Tulip's sharp brown eyes had noticed it had been left out, and he immediately asked where the door led to. "A broom cupboard," Captain Thomson had said, and hurried him on.

There was probably a reason for this which they would be told, but it did make them wonder.

"What do *you* think of Mr. Tulip?" Jemima asked Mrs. Deal, who was already dusting.

"Now don't you bother me with your questions," said Mrs. Deal, flipping and flicking. "I've never seen dust settle as it does in this place. He's a proper gentleman."

"Yes, but do you like him?" said Jemima.

"You can never tell with a fat face," said Mrs. Deal. "A fat cheek smiles whether it will or nay."

"You see, we were wondering why Captain Thomson didn't show . . ." began Jane, when Mrs. Deal arrived near her with a positive whirring of duster and mop.

"How can I get into the corners if you two great lumps are forever filling them? Move over, child."

Realizing they'd get no sense out of her, the two girls went through the Blowup Room and up the stairs to the cliff. Here an amazing scene was taking place. A large white awning decorated with red tulips had been set up on the grass. Under it was a round table laid for six, with silver and glass and a gleaming white cloth. Dozens of sailors were bustling about with buckets of ice, champagne bottles, bowls of fruit, and unloading hampers filled with pastries, jars of caviar and paté, and other delicacies. Two motor launches skimmed continually to and from the submarine, bringing more food and drink; also chairs, a swinging sofa, and iron stoves, which were immediately lit and then concealed within brightly striped tents from which the most wonderful smells soon began to waft.

When at last Jane and Jemima dragged themselves away and went down to the Mess again, the two soldiers and Mr. Tulip had returned and were in the kitchen.

"I've never seen explosive in better condition," Mr. Tulip was saying as they came in. "My dear Sergeant, you've done a magnificent job. If you ever need employment come to me. Every stick of dynamite as dry as a bone. Every block of TNT firm and solid. Now, Captain—I have a *tiny* suggestion. I could *use* that explosive. For—well, for . . ." Mr. Tulip looked for an instant rather flustered. "For various philanthropic and charitable purposes," he went on quickly. "For scientific surveys and slum clearance. For swamp destruction and famine relief schemes—you can imagine, my dears. What I propose is that I *buy* your explosive."

"*What?*" said Captain Thomson.

"Oh, don't let price worry you," said Mr. Tulip airily but swiftly. "No, no—as I said, I'm wealthy. Two hundred and fifty thousand? Pounds? Well, why not a round figure? Say half a million. Oh, my dear—what am I *quibbling* about? A million. A cool million."

At last a purple Captain Thomson managed to speak. "Mr. Tulip, sir! Mr. Tulip, sir!" he burst out. "This island is the property of His Majesty's Government. Your philanthropic plans have allowed you to become carried away. There can be no question of a sale. Sergeant Cobbin and myself hold it on trust. We have signed for it. The explosive must be returned to the proper authorities as soon as possible—every stick and box intact."

"Yesyesyesyes," said Mr. Tulip very rapidly indeed. "Quite so, quite so, quite so. I was forgetting it didn't belong to you. I completely forgot. Silly me. Oh, what a mistake. Of course you are quite right. Let's go and have lunch." And Mr. Tulip set off at a great rate for the beach staircase. Jane was about to say why didn't they go by the Blowup Room because it was quicker; indeed, she had actually said, "I say . . ." before she saw Captain Thomson shaking his head at her fiercely with his fingers on his lips.

This little unpleasantness—because in fact it was plain that Mr. Tulip had been irritated by Captain Thomson's brisk refusal to sell the explosive—was soon forgotten over lunch. They laughed and talked and drank far into the afternoon. Grouse and snails and sauces on things they had never dreamed existed flowed from the little tents all round. Sherbet (and some champagne) for the girls, lots of champagne and other wines and brandy for the grown-ups. When they had finished, Captain Thomson and Sergeant Cobbin sang several very long songs. Then Mr. Tulip had the table cleared, climbed onto it, and, to music from a gramophone which the Chinese steward had sensibly brought, showed them how to tap dance.

"Oh, dear," said Mr. Tulip, patting his stomach and climbing down at the end of the record. "So good for one. No one does it now, of course, but when I was young it was all the rage."

At about six-thirty, when they were sitting under the awning having tea and watching the sun go down, Mr. Tulip suddenly said, "My dears—I have a suggestion. I haven't enjoyed myself so much for years. Why don't you all come and stay with me aboard the *Tulip?* I'll take you to Cape Town, and we can go on enjoying each other's company. I'll put Commander Hautboyes in charge of Peeg with a party of sailors, and he can bring it along behind us."

They all looked down at their cups and saucers. No one spoke. Then Captain Thomson said, "That's a kind and generous offer, Mr. Tulip."

"Oh come, my dear," Mr. Tulip suddenly interrupted. "Call me Edward. Call me Eddie. All of you."

"Er, yes," said Captain Thomson. "Mine's Anthony. Tony. As I was saying—er, Edward, Eddie—that's a very generous offer. But on behalf of Sergeant Cobbin and myself I must reluctantly refuse. We cannot abandon our post on Peeg until we hand her over personally to the Royal Navy."

Only Mrs. Deal looked disappointed. The submarine, though not exactly a ship, and certainly not in the Royal Navy, was as near as she had been to either for a long time. She had been looking forward to a week or two on the ocean wave. However, she said, "My place is by the Captain's side, Mr. Tulip."

"Eddie," said Mr. Tulip.

"Mr. Eddie," said Mrs. Deal. "And I must insist that Miss Jemima and Miss Jane stay with me. Their parents would wish it."

Jane and Jemima were secretly delighted by this. Though they had enjoyed their little green room and the huge meals, it had all been too strange and grand. Also, they wanted to go on doing all the things they had done on Peeg before.

"Yes," said Jane, "I think we ought to stay with Mrs. Deal really."

"Very well. I see what you mean. It does you credit," said Mr. Tulip, looking suddenly rather weary and also cross. He got up and shouted to the Chinese steward, "Hoo—get the boat ready."

"Er—Eddie," said Captain Thomson awkwardly, "there is one thing you could do. If you could radio Cape Town and inform the authorities of our presence; tell them Operation Peeg is intact and ask them to inform the parents of these two girls. That would be very civil."

"And my brother in Peeblesshire," said Mrs. Deal. "I'll give you his name and address."

"Not a chance, my dears," said Mr. Tulip, looking more cheerful. "Wireless is totally out of order. Of course, I'll do it as soon as I can. Hoo—hurry up with that boat."

They said good-bye and thanked him for lunch. But Mr. Tulip still seemed quite disgruntled and left after a few brisk words. Down in the Mess, Mrs. Deal, still affected by the delicious lunch, said she thought it was due to the frustration of his charitable purposes.

"Burning as he must be with the desire to do good," she

said, "it would naturally irritate to have the chance removed."

"It's an odd charity that requires all that explosive," said Sergeant Cobbin.

"Not at all," said Mrs. Deal. "He works in a big way, clearing slums and such like. This is none of your small charity—your flags and the like."

"Maybe," said Sergeant Cobbin.

"Oh, I've no doubt the fellow's genuine, Sergeant," said Captain Thomson. "I don't think that Major Gribble of the Seventh would know a bad 'un. No—he's a bit embarrassing sometimes, but a man can behave as he wishes on his own ship I suppose. And he's been civil to us, very civil."

"He's a regular gentleman," said Mrs. Deal. "Not precisely *in* the Royal Navy, but you can tell the sea is in his blood. He runs that craft to the manner born, a perfect amateur seaman."

"It's a nice bit of engineering," said Sergeant Cobbin.

"Trim," said Mrs. Deal, "very trim I'd call it."

"Fourteen thousand three hundred and twenty tons," recited Sergeant Cobbin, "six hundred feet long, seventy feet deep, forty-five-foot beam."

"Why didn't you show him the Blowup Room?" Jane asked Captain Thomson.

"Yes—well, I thought we ought to keep something up our sleeves," said Captain Thomson. "One never knows. But I'm sure he's aboveboard."

They had a light supper of dried-egg omelet and condensed-milk pudding and then retired early to bed.

8

THE OTHER SIDE OF MR. TULIP

THE NEXT DAY began how once so many days had begun
on Peeg.

Mrs. Deal planned the largest dust she had ever under-
taken; nothing less than the entire island. Or, rather, those
parts that could be dusted: all the rooms in the Mess, the
tunnels, each explosive chamber, and the engine room.

For the first part of the morning Captain Thomson
gave Jane and Jemima a lesson called "How to give a lec-
ture." This only lasted till ten o'clock, and the two girls
then went for a walk along the cliff to see if they could
find any gulls' eggs.

"Don't go near the Peeg Special," said Captain Thomson, to whom suspicion, a strong part of his character, had
returned during the night. "They may be watching from
the *Tulip*, and I'd like to keep something else up our
sleeves."

He himself worked in his garden. There was a lot of
weeding and watering to do, and also, although the rivalry
between him and Sergeant Cobbin had grown much less
recently, he still liked to surprise Mrs. Deal with a giant
turnip from time to time, or a basket of tomatoes.

Sergeant Cobbin went to his engine room. "There's always something needs doing to an engine," he said, as he bicycled away down the tunnel.

They gathered in the kitchen again at one o'clock for lunch.

"It's good to be back at work," said Sergeant Cobbin.

"Not a moment too soon," said Mrs. Deal. "The dirt and dust in the shooting range! You wouldn't believe it."

"Some of those weeds had grown two inches," Captain Thomson said.

"Another day and me tappits would have clogged," said Sergeant Cobbin.

Jane and Jemima were pleased too, though their lessons were hardly work. Certainly, Miss Boyle would not have thought so. But there was something comforting and safe about everyone settling down to their tasks again. However, this peaceful start was interrupted in the middle of lunch. They had just finished their baked beans and sardines when there came the sound of running footsteps outside the kitchen door. It burst open and in rushed Mr. Tulip.

"My dears! Eating—how awful of me. But I have news. This morning there was a flicker of life from our wireless. Before it went dead again, I learned two things. South Africa is a tiny bit dangerous at the moment—the British base has closed. But a large naval fleet is going to visit Australia just after Christmas. Now, *mes enfants*—I have a plan. Let us attach Peeg to *Tulip*. The nuclear engines are very powerful. I should be able to tow you to Australia much sooner than you'd have reached the Cape at the rate you're going now. You, my dears, remain in charge; not so much as a *crumb* of explosive is to be moved; but you get there earlier."

Captain Thomson thought for a moment and asked

Sergeant Cobbin what he thought. Mrs. Deal said the presence of the Navy was in the plan's favor. Quite quickly they all decided the idea was a good one, and Captain Thomson gave a little speech of thanks.

"Don't mention it, my dear," Mr. Tulip interrupted halfway through. "Now if you'll excuse me, I'll set the boys to work this very moment."

When they came onto the clifftop after lunch, the whole of Peeg seemed covered in men. Among them, quite frantic with excitement, jumped, spun, sped fat Mr. Tulip.

What they were doing was hammering eight thick steel girders deep into the rock of the island. These would then be joined to the *Tulip* with steel ropes. It was very hard work. The girders bent and had to be replaced; the drills broke; the heavy machine for hammering in the girders had to be dragged to and fro. By evening the work was still not done, and it continued all night by the light of powerful lamps.

Not until lunch the next day did eight long sagging steel wires hang between Peeg and the submarine *Tulip*. To one of them a telephone cable had been attached, running into the Mess.

They all gathered on the clifftop to see the submarine start towing. At first nothing much happened, except that the sea at the back end of *Tulip* seethed and bubbled and the long drooping wire ropes tightened. But then they noticed tiny ripples spreading back from the rocks sticking up out of the sea off the beach. These grew gradually larger. Then they noticed a faint breeze blowing onto their faces off the sea. After four hours they were moving at five knots, and the submarine very slowly began to pull to the right until, after turning the island round nearly a quarter of a circle, it set off straight again, headed for Australia.

So the Island of Peeg began her last voyage. The first two weeks were very peaceful. Work on the island continued as usual. Mrs. Deal completed cleaning the Mess and began on the tunnels. At night, if a wind got up, they could hear the cables humming and throbbing. By day, seagulls sat on them. Mr. Tulip seemed very busy and preoccupied; nevertheless, he asked them to several meals and showed them some films. But he always politely refused their own invitations, saying that he had too much to do (Jane and Jemima decided that he was frightened of Mrs. Deal's cooking). Then, at the end of a fortnight, two rather strange things happened.

The first took place on one of those days they were having lunch on the *Tulip*. Jane had a bad cold and a temperature, so Mrs. Deal said she must spend the day in bed. Jemima had gone for a long walk in the morning to see if she could find some wild flowers for Jane's room. This is not so surprising as it sounds, for Peeg had started to change from the desert it had become on their journey south. Not only had the weather been getting colder, but twice recently there had been a little rain.

Lunch with Mr. Tulip was rather boring, at least for Jemima. He produced several bottles of what he said was a special wine, which she of course didn't drink. But the others had quite a lot. Even Mrs. Deal said, "Well, if you *insist*, Mr. Tulip." (They had all long ago given up trying to call him Eddie or even Edward.)

After lunch they were all talking so much that Jemima slipped out of the dining room. She suddenly thought she would explore the submarine. She and Jane had discussed only the day before how odd it was that they had never looked at any part of it without Mr. Tulip or Commander Hautboyes being there to show it to them. No one seemed to have noticed that she had left the dining room, so it seemed an ideal opportunity to explore. Jemima slipped through another door and in a moment was off down a long steel corridor.

For over an hour she wandered down one corridor after another, up and down steel ladders and lifts. She saw the kitchen, a billiards room, and the little cabins with six bunks each where the crew slept. Normally she would have been too nervous to do this sort of thing without Jane, but in fact it wasn't at all difficult. She started off imagining what she would say if anyone stopped her, but the sailors stepped politely aside to let her pass and one of them saluted her. Also, Jemima was rather pleased that she would have something to tell Jane.

At last, however, she thought she'd seen enough. Her legs were tired, and she felt it must be getting late. She was about to ask the way back to the stateroom when she saw a steel door with a notice on it saying NO ADMITTANCE. At once, her heart beating, she gave it a tiny push. To her horror it immediately and easily swung open.

Jemima knew that Jane would have gone in. How exciting to be able to go back and tell Jane that that was what she had done. Hoping that a sailor might appear and say, "Hey—you can't go in there," Jemima very slowly walked toward the open door.

No sailor came. She was standing in an enormous chamber, larger even than the stateroom. It was as wide as the submarine and must have been about forty feet high. Down both sides, tilted at a slight angle, there was a row of large rockets. Each rocket had US AIR FORCE printed on it, and each pointed nose, which she could just see high above her in the semidarkness, rested against a round bolted trap in the side of the submarine.

What were they? Perhaps, thought Jemima nervously,

they were atomic rockets. She walked slowly up the large dim chamber, the twenty-four rockets (twelve in each row) standing in silent ranks as she passed. Why should Mr. Tulip want twenty-four atomic rockets? Perhaps they were something to do with weather and he only planned to fire them up into the clouds to see how hot they were or wet or something. But somehow they looked more frightening than this, too sharp and fat and long.

At the far end of the chamber there were two large panels in the wall covered with dials and knobs and other instruments. She was examining these when she heard a dull clang and then the sound of echoing voices.

Coming toward her from the steel door she saw Mr. Tulip and a tall, elderly man in white overalls she had never seen before. Luckily they were talking so hard they did not notice her, and she was able to hide behind the tail fins of the nearest rocket.

"Well, I still haven't decided, *mon brave*," Mr. Tulip was saying. "I've alerted all those who might be concerned. But you know the problems, Dr. Interdenze, as well as I do, don't you?"

"Certainly, sir," said Dr. Interdenze, in a strong German accent.

"We could certainly equip these objects," Mr. Tulip said, waving a fat hand vaguely at the rockets.

"I haf worked out plans for them, sir," said Dr. Interdenze.

They began to talk about things Jemima simply could not follow. Crouching down among the tail fins of her rocket, she noticed that though Mr. Tulip made his usual silly jokes he was in fact rather quicker and brisker. He asked a lot of short questions. Dr. Interdenze was very polite; indeed, he seemed rather frightened of Mr. Tulip.

Perhaps it was this that kept Jemima hiding. She did

not quite know why she had hidden in the first place, and she had meant to come out and surprise Mr. Tulip after a few minutes. But now she decided to try to creep away without being seen. Somehow she had left it too late; also, there was something a bit different about Mr. Tulip, something a bit frightening.

Very carefully, she slipped along to the next rocket. The men went on talking. She tiptoed to the next and then the next and soon was quite near the door. She could see Mr. Tulip and Dr. Interdenze standing with their backs to her looking at the panels. The next moment she was in the corridor again.

One of the sailors took her back to the stateroom where she found Commander Hautboyes, who told her that the others had gone back to Peeg some time ago. He didn't seem very interested in what she had been doing and at once had her put on a boat and taken back to the island.

Jemima arrived in the Mess just as Sergeant Cobbin and Captain Thomson were about to set off on some expedition.

"Stop!" she cried. "I've found out something very odd." As fast, but as carefully as she could, she told them everything. Everyone listened in complete silence. Jane, whose bed had been put in the anteroom so that she could be near the telephone, got out of it and came and stood nearer so that she could hear.

"Goodness, how *brave*," she said to Jemima when she'd finished. "I wouldn't have dared. Weren't you scared stiff?"

"Well, I was a bit," said Jemima, feeling very pleased and proud. "But I was quite safe. I'm sure Mr. Tulip would never hurt me. They're probably weather rockets."

"Well, I think you're very brave," said Jane, putting her arm round Jemima's shoulders.

"You've done very well," said Captain Thomson in a grave voice. "This is very interesting. The rockets *may*, as you say, be weather rockets, but they may not. You say Tulip said he had alerted all those who might be concerned? Now that may mean weather stations, but it may not. Certainly, if the submarine is a weather ship, why didn't he tell us? And if he can alert people it shows his wireless is really working. Forewarned is forearmed. Sergeant, go and see that the Peeg Special is loaded with petrol. See that it is well hidden. I will go and check the mechanisms in the Blowup Room. Mrs. Deal, Jemima, stay with me; Jane, get back to bed. We must all get fighting fit."

The change in the two soldiers was considerable. That evening they both changed into what Captain Thomson called patrol kit—which consisted of big loose jackets painted various autumn colors, tight trousers, things like large stockings on their heads—and covered their faces in boot polish. They disappeared dressed like this after dinner and didn't get back until everyone else had long been asleep. Before they had set out, Captain Thomson had started to read a small pamphlet called *In Enemy Territory*.

The second strange thing occurred at the beginning of the third week. It was a gray, blustery day with low clouds. Sergeant Cobbin, Captain Thomson, Jane, and Jemima were standing on the clifftop watching the *Tulip* plow through heavy seas; the long cables connecting her to the island hummed and vibrated and were often buried by large waves.

Captain Thomson suddenly said, "It's been getting cold very quickly. What direction have we been heading, Sergeant?"

"I ain't certain," said Sergeant Cobbin, "but I'd reckon we'd have been going south."

"That's what I feel," said Captain Thomson. "Yet Australia is more southeast surely. Something odd here."

"I can check easy enough," said Sergeant Cobbin. "I'll just go and have a look at the old compass in me engine room."

In half an hour he was back, red, panting, and dramatic. "It's gone!" he said, pointing toward the engine room.

"Gone?" said Captain Thomson. "How do you mean, gone? What's gone?"

"Me compass has bin took," said Sergeant Cobbin, sounding very Suffolk. "Someone's bin and unscrewed it from the old binnacle and took it."

"I see," said Captain Thomson slowly. "Someone—presumably under Mr. Tulip's orders—has taken our compass. Things get stranger and stranger. We must plan our strategy and our tactics. Sergeant Cobbin—O Group tonight at eight-thirty. Things are coming to a head."

But for some days nothing new happened. It got colder and wetter, and in the evenings they lit the iron stove in the anteroom and took hot-water bottles to bed with them. The more it rained, the more Peeg changed. Shoots of heather appeared and a lot of moss, which had seemed completely dead, suddenly came alive. A thin trickle of water ran down the middle of the burn again. Several times Sergeant Cobbin and Captain Thomson got up in the middle of the night, put on their patrol kit, covered their faces in boot polish, and disappeared until morning. Jane and Jemima couldn't imagine what they were doing, and when they got back at breakfast time the two soldiers were too tired to be asked questions.

Then, suddenly, at the beginning of the second month they found out the whole terrible truth.

It was one of the first fairly calm days that they'd had for a week. In the morning Mr. Tulip rang them up and asked them if they'd like to come over for a game of Ping-Pong before tea. They had done this quite often before Jemima's discovery, and the soldiers had both enjoyed it. Captain Thomson said that, though circumstances were different now, that was all the more reason for going. On no account should they rouse Mr. Tulip's suspicions.

Mr. Tulip himself was, as usual now, too busy to play. But a number of other officers at once challenged Captain Thomson and Sergeant Cobbin to a match. Normally the others sat and watched the men play about seventy games. Sometimes Jane and Jemima were allowed one game at the very end. This time, however, Jane whispered to Jemima, "Say I've gone for a walk if anybody asks," and quietly slipped out of the sports room while everyone was settling down.

Captain Thomson had been reading in *In Enemy Territory* aloud to them all in the evenings. Jane walked slowly and innocently, whistling and smiling. "Keep your eyes open," Captain Thomson had said. "But don't ask questions."

For a while she saw nothing. The submarine hummed and quivered as it plunged on through the sea. Sailors bustled about their business, receiving huge innocent smiles whenever they passed Jane.

She was about to turn back, when she turned a corner and saw, halfway down a short stretch of corridor, two *Tulip* sailors with rifles over their shoulders standing guard by a door.

This was certainly unusual. Jane sauntered up to them and, forgetting Captain Thomson's orders, said, "Could you tell me, please, what happens in there?"

"Clear off," said the sailor roughly. "Mr. Tulip's orders. No one's allowed round here."

This, too, was unusual. Normally the sailors were very polite, and Mr. Tulip was always saying that he wanted them to look on the whole submarine as their home. However, feeling very cunning, Jane just walked slowly away, saying vaguely, "How interesting."

"Get a move on," shouted the sailor.

"All right, all right—keep your hair on," said Jane crossly, hurrying round the corner.

Once out of sight, however, she slowed down again. This was clearly extremely suspicious. Even the rockets hadn't been guarded. Quite obviously she must get into the room behind that door—but how? There were no windows and no other doors, just the bare steel walls and the usual bundle of pipes and wires running along under the ceiling.

It was the sight of the pipes and wires which gave her an idea. They ran everywhere all over the submarine, and every so often, where they disappeared into a bulkhead or steel wall, there would be a small square door high up with INSPECTION POINT written on it. Jane ran down to the end of the corridor—a short one—and there sure enough she found one, with steel rungs set in the wall. With a quick look round to see that no one was coming, she climbed the rungs and pushed at the door.

It opened onto a long, low place like a deep, narrow cupboard. Jane crawled quickly in and pulled the little door shut behind her.

She could only lie on her stomach. By the light of a faint pale blue bulb she saw a maze of pipes and wires, which ran into a lot of boxes with dials and knobs on. But far more exciting than this was the faint but definite sound of voices; a burring she could hear above the humming of the submarine. Jane wriggled to the end of the inspection point and saw at the corner a ring of light round two pipes that disappeared into the room on the other side. Lying flat, she put her eye to the crack.

She saw a small bit of a round table. Sitting at it, in full view, was Commander Hautboyes; on his right she saw half of a tall thin man she did not recognize; and to the left she could just see the hands of Mr. Tulip, with his large red ring on a fat forefinger. Everything else was cut off by the edge of the hole, but she could tell by the murmur of voices that several more people were sitting there. She found that by putting her ear to the crack she could hear quite well.

". . . I would like," said the tall thin man.

She heard Mr. Tulip say distinctly, "I'm sure you would—wouldn't we all?" Then she saw him smack one plump hand firmly on the table.

"To business," he said. "I've called you here today to tell you something really rather thrilling. Interdenze and myself have finally completed our plans for the Island of Peeg."

With a jump of excitement, Jane realized she must be going to find out what some of the mysterious happenings meant. She pressed her ear to the little opening.

"As you know," went on Mr. Tulip, "this innocent island is loaded with some eight million tons of TNT and other explosive. The equivalent of two or three hydrogen bombs. My plan is very simple. In a month's time we will have towed Peeg to the Ross Ice Shelf. Now, Interdenze, before I go on, just give a very brief résumé of what would happen if we were to explode the island beside the Ross Ice Shelf."

Jane heard a scraping of chairs and a clearing of throats. Then the thin man said, "An explosion of this magnitude would subject four or five square miles to searing heat and devastating disturbance. First an immense tidal wave, some hundred miles long and one hundred feet high, would sweep out over the ocean. It would reach Tasmania in three days at a height of approximately forty feet. The coastal regions would be devastated. Loss of life and property would be catastrophic.

"The second result of exploding Peeg is more interesting. A vast area of the Ross Ice Shelf will be detached. Millions of tons of ice, in the form of huge icebergs, will be carried first northwest by the prevailing currents and then, when they meet the Roaring Forties, back onto Australia. Our computers estimate that over a period of two years the temperature along the whole of southern Australia will drop 30° Fahrenheit. It is true to say that Australia will be crippled."

"Vivid," said Mr. Tulip. "Now, gentlemen—when we have placed the Island of Peeg against the ice shelf the submarine *Tulip* will immediately proceed to the Indian Ocean. I shall instruct the Australian government to drop five hundred million pounds sterling—or say twelve thousand million dollars—in the form of gold bullion into the ocean at a particular place. I shall warn them that all ships must be cleared round the area to a distance of one thousand miles for one week while we recover the gold and make our escape. I shall warn them that if the area is entered, which our radar can easily detect, I shall explode the island. They will hardly wish to blow it up themselves, but if so much as an Australian mosquito lands on it, I shall immediately explode it. The instruments to detect entry and to explode are at this moment being secretly installed on Peeg."

A voice said, "Can the Australian government afford five hundred million pounds?"

"They can't afford not to afford it, my dear," said Mr. Tulip. "They will borrow it."

"Suppose they send a rocket into the Indian Ocean and destroy us," someone else said.

"Destroying *Tulip* will automatically set off the exploding mechanism," said Mr. Tulip.

"What will we do with the Peeg party?" said a third invisible voice.

"Ah, me," said Mr. Tulip, spreading his hands. "You know how tenderhearted I am, my dear. I've grown quite fond of the two little girls. I shall offer them positions in the organization. I am afraid they will refuse. We will have to leave them on their island."

Soon after this they left. Jane heard them all pushing back their chairs and, peering through the crack, saw bits of them move about and then disappear. She found she was trembling, and she felt a mixture of excitement, fear, and importance. Her chin ached where it had been pressing against the pipe. She must tell Captain Thomson quickly. They must stop Mr. Tulip. But how? What could they do against so many tough men with rockets and guns and a huge submarine?

She crawled back to the door and down into the corridor. When she got back to the others they had finished playing Ping-Pong and were standing about talking. Mr. Tulip was there too, beaming and bouncing, his usual talkative self.

"And how's this little darling?" he said, trying to ruffle her hair.

Jane moved sharply away, causing Captain Thomson to frown fiercely at her.

"Quite well, Mr. Tulip," she said. She felt frightened of

him and thought he must somehow be able to tell that she had overheard him just by her expression.

Jemima noticed at once that something was wrong and, coming beside her, said, "What's happened?"

"Nothing," Jane whispered. "Sssh. I'll tell you later."

"My dears—we must see more of each other. I've neglected you in the last few days. Come to supper—tomorrow, Captain?"

"Splendid," said Captain Thomson heartily. "Excellent. We'd love that. Very good of you."

Soon afterward they left, Jane managing to avoid Mr. Tulip's kiss. It was foggy and quite cold out on the sea, but not rough. At first they could not see Peeg at all, but just the black, dripping cables disappearing ahead of them.

The moment they arrived in the Mess, Captain Thomson turned to Jane, his big kind face red and cross. "Now, Jane, I'm most displeased," he said. "I've told you how important it is not to arouse Mr. Tulip's suspicions. You must let Mr. Tulip pinch you and ruffle your hair. He's the pinching sort."

"But don't you see?" said Jemima. "Something's happened."

"What?" said Captain Thomson.

Jane paused, feeling very dramatic. Then she said, "I know what Mr. Tulip is going to do."

She couldn't remember all the details, like the name of the ice shelf, but she remembered quite enough to convince them of the really terrible danger. No one spoke, except Mrs. Deal, who cried at regular intervals, "No!" and "I can't believe it!"

When she'd finished, Jemima, who was still holding her arm, said, "Goodness—weren't you terrified? You see—I knew you'd be just as brave."

"And him a naval man, or at least a man of the sea," said Mrs. Deal. "I can hardly credit it."

"I'm afraid it's true," said Captain Thomson, who was looking extremely grim. "Not that Mr. Tulip wishes to kill us. I imagine that he supposes the Australians will be willing to pay up and that after an uncomfortable time we will be rescued. But that this is his plan I have no doubt. There have been other indications. Not only the rockets Jemima discovered, but other signs—have there not, Sergeant Cobbin?"

There was no answer. "Sergeant Cobbin?" said Captain Thomson sharply. "Where's Sergeant Cobbin?"

"He's gone!" cried Mrs. Deal. "Oh, mercy me. They're snatching us up one by one. We'll be taken in our beds. Come here, Jane, Jemima."

However, in a few minutes Sergeant Cobbin came through the door. "She's right," he said. "Just bin taking a look down the old tunnel. Someone's fixed a length of new wire right along the roof. They'd hidden it well, but I seed it soon enough."

"Now," said Captain Thomson, "we are dealing with a dangerous man. He is certainly rather mad. No one but a madman could contemplate such a deed. Luckily, Sergeant Cobbin and I have worked out various plans for various situations. I think Plan D would fill the bill, don't you, Sergeant?"

"She'd fit it a treat," said Sergeant Cobbin.

"Will we have to put boot polish on our faces?" said Jane, giggling.

Captain Thomson looked at her rather coldly, then went on, "The details of the plan are not quite worked out. We'll do that tonight, Sergeant."

That night, before they went to sleep, the two girls

talked and talked, discussing Mr. Tulip, trying to think of their own plan.

"We could all get into the Peeg Special—fly away," said Jemima.

"But would it hold us all?" said Jane. "And where would we fly to. And how far? And, anyway, I expect he'd shoot us down with one of his guns."

"Well, what?" said Jemima.

"We could tip the boxes of explosive one by one secretly into the sea at night," said Jane.

"Eight million tons?" said Jemima. "It would take ages."

"Yes, I suppose so—weeks, anyway."

"Years," said Jemima.

In the end they couldn't think what was to be done. "We must just hope Plan D is good," said Jane.

"He was awfully cross when you said boot polish," said Jemima.

"I know," said Jane, "but honestly—I mean it makes them both look so silly, and they never get it all off. I'd have thought seeing boot polish behind their ears would be enough to make Mr. Tulip suspicious. He must think they're mad, if you ask me."

The next morning after breakfast Captain Thomson gathered everyone in the anteroom to explain Plan D.

It was simple but brilliant. That very day they would ask Mr. Tulip to supper. He never came over with more than two or three sailors, and these just used to sit and gossip in the kitchen with Mrs. Deal. Halfway through supper in the anteroom, Sergeant Cobbin would leave the table on some pretext, go through to the kitchen—picking up a machine gun on the way—and hold up the sailors. Mrs. Deal would tie them up. And they would then have Mr. Tulip in their power and be able to dictate terms.

There seemed only one drawback. "We have asked Mr. Tulip to supper at least nine times," said Jane, "and he's always refused."

"Oh, don't worry about that," said Captain Thomson confidently. "I wasn't Mess Secretary for nothing in the good old days, you know. I'll turn on the charm."

After lunch Captain Thomson settled himself at the telephone. Quite soon he was engaged in a rather difficult conversation.

"Mr. Tulip? Ah—Thomson here . . . Very well, thank you. And you? . . . Good . . . Look, there's been a bit of a chinwag here about coming over for supper tonight. We feel you should come here, sir. We'd like to invite *you* to supper. Just a snack. Dress informal."

There was a silence while Captain Thomson listened. Then he said, "No, no, Mr. Tulip. We'll take no excuse. We insist. It's our turn, old fellow."

Again Mr. Tulip must have refused. Again Captain Thomson insisted. Again and again and again Mr. Tulip refused. Captain Thomson began to look rather red; he begged and pleaded; after a while he charmed.

"Look—er—Edward—er—Eddie—think nothing of it, old man. My dear chap—it's humble fare, I know, but for you—er—Eddie—dear chap . . ." He asked Mr. Tulip to tea. He asked him to come and have a sandwich. He asked him to come and have drinks. A drink.

In the end he became quite desperate. "Look here, Tulip," he said. "It's a question of hospitality. As an English gentleman, you'll understand I really don't feel we can come to you again—we won't come to you again until you've come to us. It's a matter of etiquette, an Englishman's honor."

In the end Mr. Tulip agreed to come and have a drink with them that evening provided they all then had dinner on the submarine. Captain Thomson mopped his forehead, exhausted but triumphant.

"You see," he said to Jane and Jemima, "I knew I'd persuade him."

"Force him, you mean," said Jane. "Don't you think he'll suspect something?"

"Oh, good gracious no," said Captain Thomson. "He understands. He may be a villain, but he's a gentleman. That is, he knows how gentlemen behave."

Captain Thomson was right. Promptly at six o'clock Mr. Tulip appeared at the Mess. He was wearing a clean white uniform sparingly embroidered with scarlet tulips, and carried a light malacca cane with a tulip made of some large red stone on its top. A ruby, he explained to Jemima, a bit of foolishness he'd had made for him in Bombay.

They had spent all afternoon rehearsing what to do. The first drink was to be served from rather a small jug. When it ran out, Captain Thomson was to ask Sergeant Cobbin to get some more. On the way he would collect his machine gun from the cupboard outside the kitchen. While he kept the sailors covered with the gun, Mrs. Deal would tie them up. They would be gagged and left with Mrs. Deal, to whom Sergeant Cobbin would give his gun. Sergeant Cobbin would then return to the anteroom and blow his nose twice if everything was all right. This would be a signal for Captain Thomson to go to a drawer and say, "I think these would interest you, Mr. Tulip," producing two more guns, one of which he would toss to Sergeant Cobbin. They would then discuss terms with Mr. Tulip. If more than four sailors appeared or if Mr. Tulip showed any signs of being suspicious, then the whole of Plan D was to be immediately abandoned.

But in fact only two sailors appeared and Mr. Tulip was gaiety and politeness itself. He smiled and giggled; he told amusing stories about a sailor called Bill being rude to Commander Hautboyes, and another called Raphael being rude to someone they hadn't met called Herr Interdenze (Jane and Jemima exchanged a quick look). He laughed and laughed and was eventually almost weeping with laughter, with his fat round white hand on Captain Thomson's stiff bony knee, and crying out, "Oh, my dear! My dear—you simply wouldn't *believe* the goings-on."

There had been some trouble over the drink. All they had left was two bottles of rum, but Mrs. Deal had cleverly made a punch by mixing this with lemonade crystals, sugar, and hot water. It tasted, Jane and Jemima thought, delicious—very sweet, boiling hot, and very strong.

They had been talking happily about this and that for about a quarter of an hour when Captain Thomson said in a casual voice, "Oh, Sergeant, the jug's empty. Go and get some more, will you?"

"Not on my account, my dear," said Mr. Tulip hurriedly. "I have ample, ample." He held up his glass, which was indeed still almost full.

"Nonsense nonsense," said Captain Thomson. "Nonsense—er, Eddie. Drink up, sir. Off you go, Sergeant."

"Right you are, sir," said Sergeant Cobbin. They heard him clump off toward the kitchen.

A silence fell. Jane's heart was beating, and she tried hard to hear the sounds of a struggle in the kitchen. Even Captain Thomson seemed under strain. He was brick red and kept on pulling his moustache. Someone must speak, thought Jane.

"Did you sleep well last night, Mr. Tulip?" she said at last.

"Well, I had a rather restless night, my dear," said Mr. Tulip. "A touch restless. And you?"

"Very restless," said Jane. Then, thinking this might

sound suspicious, she added quickly, "Very restless at first, then very calm."

Captain Thomson cleared his throat. "Where were we?" he said loudly. "What was I saying?"

"Nothing, my dear," said Mr. Tulip.

Captain Thomson pulled his moustache. "It's been restless weather—er, Edward—Eddie. Normal for these latitudes, I suppose?"

"I haven't the faintest idea," said Mr. Tulip. "I don't even know what latitude we're in. I leave all that to my navigators."

There was another silence. Jane could hardly bear it. Captain Thomson said suddenly, "Where the hell's Cobbin?"

And then the door opened and in came Sergeant Cobbin. He was smiling and carrying a jug. He put it down and pulling out his handkerchief blew his nose twice, very loudly.

Captain Thomson tried to fill Mr. Tulip's glass. When he was waved politely away he said, "I've got something here I think would interest you, Tulip."

He walked over to the table and stood for a moment with his back to them. Then he opened a drawer, picked something up, and, whirling round, pointed the gun at Mr. Tulip's chest.

"It's this," he said. "Right, Tulip, I'm afraid the game's up. Raise your hands above your head and stand up. I shall not hesitate to shoot."

Behind him, Sergeant Cobbin had taken the second gun and moved to where he could keep it pointing at Mr. Tulip.

Mr. Tulip said, "Careful, my dear—those old weapons, terribly dicey."

"I mean it, Tulip," said Captain Thomson.

But Mr. Tulip did not move. He seemed quite unconcerned. He looked calmly at the two soldiers and then said rather coldly, "Look—you don't think I didn't know about this, do you? I'm not a ninny, you know." Suddenly he raised his head and, turning it to the door, he cried out, "Haut*boyes!* *Haut*boyes—HAUTBOYES!"

Immediately the anteroom appeared to be full of sailors. Led by Commander Hautboyes, they poured in, ten, fifteen, twenty of them, heavily armed and very tall and strong. Before Captain Thomson and Sergeant Cobbin could move they were seized and thrown to the floor. Jane saw a huge sailor seize Jemima and was then seized herself.

"I shall see them in the stateroom in an hour," said Mr. Tulip. "Don't be too rough with the girls." He bowed to Captain Thomson and Sergeant Cobbin, who were almost buried by struggling sailors. "Thanks for a delicious drink," he said, and then daintily tripped out of the door.

They had been waiting in the stateroom for a quarter of an hour. Captain Thomson and Sergeant Cobbin were tightly bound at the wrists; Jane and Jemima and Mrs. Deal were free. Two sailors with rifles stood guard. No one spoke, though now and again a quiet sob came from Jemima, who was sitting very frightened on Mrs. Deal's lap.

At last the door into the dining room opened and Mr. Tulip appeared, somehow rather in the same way as when they'd first met him. He sat down at the table and beckoned them over. The two guards followed them and stood behind the two soldiers when they sat down.

"Well, I'm sorry it's happened like this, my dears," said Mr. Tulip. "I hate unpleasantness—but you left me with no choice really, did you?"

"How did you find out we'd found out?" said Jane.

"My dear—the first thing I did was to have the Mess bugged," said Mr. Tulip. "If that's not a vulgar way of putting it. Little microphones in every room, Captain. They've developed a lot since your day. I've heard everything. I heard when Jemima found the rockets. I heard about your little prank, Jane. I could have taken you all then, but I was interested in what you'd do.

"Now—I've a lot to do. I shall make you this offer. I can give you all positions in my organization. You two girls I would take under my wing. I would like you to think of me as a father. What do you say?"

"I can answer for us all," said Captain Thomson. "I don't know what your organization is or what it does, but the answer is NO."

"I feared you'd say that," said Mr. Tulip. "Well—the alternative, I'm afraid, may be unpleasant, though I certainly hope not. It all depends how sensible the Australian government is."

"You are quite obviously mad," said Captain Thomson. "Do you suppose the Australian government will do anything but ignore your mad messages?"

"My dear," said Mr. Tulip, "you don't actually know a great deal about me, do you? Because I have a—well, slightly theatrical way of talking, you imagine I'm only acting, don't you? A lot of people have underestimated me for much the same reason. Let me explain a few things to you in about thirty seconds.

"I am the head of an extremely powerful organization called Pilut," he began, and suddenly, though he looked no different, Jane felt frightened of him. He seemed cold and hard and somehow dangerous. His light jokes, his affected way of talking, instead of being rather foolish, now appeared as disguises for someone very clever and very scheming.

"My name," Mr. Tulip went on, "is in fact Pilut. I am a Hungarian of ancient family born and brought up in England."

"I thought you said your family owned a nickel mine in Australia," said Jane.

"So I did, darling," said Mr. Tulip rather sarcastically. "What makes you think that Hungarians can't own nickel mines in Australia?"

Jane didn't answer, and after a moment Mr. Tulip went on. "In the last ten years Pilut has been partially or largely responsible for the Cuban Revolution, the race riots in America, and the Arab-Israeli wars. Also robberies and forgeries too numerous to mention. None of this, of course, our good soldiers will understand. It all happened while they were, somewhat ridiculously I can't help feeling, cooped up inside Peeg waiting to fight in a war which had ended ten or fifteen years before."

Captain Thomson did not answer this insult, but Jane saw Sergeant Cobbin clench his large fists.

"Pilut has been responsible for a great deal of lucrative crime and national disturbance. Our name is kept hidden by governments seeking to destroy us. But they also pay us. Last year, for instance, Pilut made a profit of three million pounds." Mr. Tulip was silent. And looking at him, Jane was suddenly reminded of a film she had seen.

"I think you're just making it up," she said all at once. "It's too childish. It's just like a James Bond film I saw once."

The effect of this was quite extraordinary. Staring at her, Mr. Tulip slowly stood up. He grew whiter and whiter and began to tremble. For ten seconds he was unable to speak, and then, suddenly leaning across at her, he screamed at the top of his voice, "DO YOU THINK IAN

COULD HAVE WRITTEN HIS BOOKS WITHOUT ME?"

Jane didn't answer.

"DO YOU?" screamed Mr. Tulip.

Jane was too terrified even to look at him. But Mr. Tulip was now striding up and down the stateroom in a frenzy of rage, jumping up and down, trembling.

"Of course he couldn't," he cried. "I *made* Fleming. My existence, which he discovered by nefarious means, inspired him. It was through his villains that he came to his hero. But to go unrecognized for what Ian stole from me is the least of my worries. A humble Pilut—yes, humble, not rich. I claw my way to the top. I sell my soul, my body, my life to achieve power, and what—still I am paid like a tradesman. I shall be recognized. The world must cringe . . . how dare they . . . Pilut . . . my childhood . . ."

They watched in amazement as Mr. Tulip became more and more disjointed and incoherent. From a scream his voice fell until it was choked with tears and they could barely hear what he was muttering. Eventually he managed to calm himself down and came slowly back to the table, looking suddenly very tired.

Captain Thomson said, "What will you do with five hundred million pounds?"

"I haven't decided," said Mr. Tulip wearily. "I shall equip twenty or thirty more Tulips. Those rockets Jemima discovered are empty; I shall buy atomic warheads for them. I shall attain the status of a great power without possessing a country or territory of any sort. Nothing but an immensely powerful navy. It is an interesting idea."

He stared at his plump fingers and became lost in thought. After a long silence, Captain Thomson stood up and cleared his throat. He said that he personally felt sorry for Mr. Tulip. It was plain that he was deranged. Nevertheless, if even one tenth of what he had said was true, he was plainly also a dangerous blackguard. He, Captain Thomson, would do his best to see Mr. Tulip was brought to justice for his crimes. He said a great many other things too. Then Mrs. Deal got up and said that, though she hadn't fully followed the discussion, she thought she felt sorry for Mr. Tulip too; nevertheless, she had come to the conclusion that, though apparently not technically in the Royal Navy, he was still a disgrace to the traditions of the sea.

Mr. Tulip didn't answer, but just stared at his fingers. He looked gloomy, his fat mouth sucked into a tiny bud. Jane was reminded of his expression when he'd once lost at Ping-Pong. That reminded her of the time they'd first seen him, and how he'd tap danced on the table and re-fused to go swimming, and all the lunches they'd eaten in the dining room. She realized she'd grown very fond of him, even of his absurd way of talking and his jokes.

"We liked you so much, Mr. Tulip," she said. "At least *I* liked you. Please don't try and blow up the ice, please be nice like you used to be. I don't want not to like you. Please, Mr. Tulip."

"Please, Mr. Tulip," said Jemima.

Mr. Tulip looked up at them and stared without speaking. He looked very sad. At last he spoke.

"You don't understand, my dear, what it's like for people like me—if there is anyone else like me. There are things we can't control even if we wanted to." He stood up and walked slowly to the door. Then without looking back he said, "Take them away."

They were each locked up in separate explosive storerooms on the island. The sailors were not too gentle.

Jane was thrown onto the beach and then dragged along by her hands. She heard Jemima cry out somewhere to her left, and when Sergeant Cobbin, who was close enough to be seen in the semidarkness, shouted at the sailors, she saw one of them hit him on the side of his head with his fist.

It was hard and uncomfortable in the storeroom. They had turned the light off, and there was just one blanket. Jane felt frightened and lonely. She didn't know where the others were. She suddenly longed for her mother and father to come and get her. Trying not to cry, she wrapped the blanket round her and lay down against one of the long wooden boxes and at last went off to sleep.

9

THE LAST EXPLOSION

FOR A WEEK the Island of Peeg continued to move steadily southeast toward the Ross Ice Shelf. The weather grew worse and at night, huddled in her blanket, Jane thought she could hear the sea pounding upon the rocks.

She never saw any of the others. Three times a day rather plain meals were brought to her on a tray. Every morning a guard would take her for an exercise walk on the cliff—three times along and back.

There were several guards, who took it in turn. Most were not very nice, one in particular being surly and silent. But one was younger and quite nice. He told her that Mr. Tulip had helped him escape from a prison in America. He was so grateful that he'd joined the Pilut organization. He said the life was exciting and the pay good, but that he missed his mother.

"You're lucky," he told Jane. "Them two soldiers there is tied up, and Sergeant Cobbin can't smoke, which he hates."

"Is Jemima all right?" Jane asked.

"She's better than she was," said the sailor. "She don't cry near so much."

"How's Mrs. Deal?" said Jane.

"Weepy," said the sailor, "weepy at first. But she's completely changed since we gave her a duster."

Twice Commander Hautboyes came in and asked her if she'd changed her mind and would like to join the Pilut organization. She said no. Her nice guard said that the others were visited by Mr. Tulip.

"He really admires that Captain," he said. "He'd sure like to get him on our team."

Jane wondered why Mr. Tulip didn't visit her. "He fears my persuasive tongue," she thought.

It grew colder. She had to wear a coat for exercise, and at the end of the week there was half an inch of snow. The Island of Peeg shone under the gray skies and looked as it used to look in the winter term.

"Three more weeks and they say we'll be at the ice shelf," said the nice guard. "Then the fun begins."

Jane had, of course, thought of escaping the moment she was thrown into the storeroom. But it did not take her long to see that she had no chance at all. The storeroom was hollowed out of the solid pumice stone and filled from floor to ceiling with heavy wooden boxes of explosive. There was only a small passage between the boxes, stretching from the door to the wall, and here Jane had to sit on a small chair or lie on her blanket. After the first night, the light was left on all the time, coming from a feeble bulb in the middle of the ceiling.

Many times during those first long, boring days she got up and minutely searched the rock face. She looked all over the ceiling to see if there were any cracks or holes she could enlarge. There was nothing.

It was the cold weather that made Jane think of escaping again. Though snow fell every day now, it never grew any colder in the storeroom. She still only needed one blanket and wore exactly the same clothes as when she'd come in. It was, she realized, the ventilation. She suddenly remembered Sergeant Cobbin telling them about the fat tubes which carried dry air at the right temperature to every single explosive store. Immediately she began to look for her tube.

By climbing up the wooden boxes, she found that there was a small gap between the top ones and the place where the ceiling curved in its middle. She pushed her way down the gap, her back scraping against the rocky ceiling, until she reached the wall. She found that the boxes had not been packed quite tight against the wall. There was a gap of as much as ten inches, often more than a foot, between the wall and the boxes. By wriggling and pushing with first her tummy and then her knees and feet against the boxes and her back to the wall, Jane began to force a way down.

By evening she had reached the floor on the far side of the boxes and found, about a foot above it, the metal grill which led to her ventilation tube. She could put her hands through the grill and feel the warm air streaming through. She couldn't quite remember how wide Sergeant Cobbin had said the tubes were, but she seemed to remember they were quite big.

She struggled up again and went back to wait in front of the door for her supper. Her shirt was torn and she'd scratched her face and hands quite badly on splinters and nails on the boxes. When the guard, one of the surly ones, came in he was quite surprised.

"What yer bin doing then?" he asked suspiciously.

"I sleepwalk, you know," said Jane quickly. "I walked in my sleep last night and spent all the time banging into those boxes and scraping against them."

"I see," said the guard, who was obviously rather stupid. "Well—don't do it again." He banged down some plain boiled fish and a suet pudding and walked out.

Jane waited until the plates had been collected and then climbed up the boxes again and down the other side. She soon found that though she could get her hands through the vents in the tube she could do nothing else. But after feeling about for a while she found a small loose nut on the inside. After undoing this she was able to pull up a corner of the vent and make a small opening. The tops of many of the boxes were loose, and Jane was easily able to break off a wooden strut and use it as a lever. Two hours' hard work, often with loud tinny noises which made her stop and listen, and she had wrenched quite a large opening in the ventilation tube—just large enough for her to squeeze through.

She felt much too tired to do that at once, so she decided to set off the next night when she was completely rested.

The day passed quicker than usual. Although, of course, excited, Jane also felt rather frightened at the idea of escaping, especially into a narrow tube. She wanted to put it off. But far too soon supper was eaten and the surly guard had locked the door.

The moment his footsteps had died away, Jane plumped her blanket so that it would look as though she was still under it. It was quite difficult getting into the ventilation tube, but eventually she was lying flat out, her arms ahead, her legs pointing toward the rushing air. She had decided that the sailors would have put her and Jemima and Mrs. Deal in the storerooms farthest from the Mess, since they would have wanted to keep Sergeant Cobbin and Captain Thomson as close to them as possible. She also decided that the warm air came from the engine room. Therefore, to go toward the Mess and away from the engine room she must move in the same direction as the air. Then she would be bound to pass Captain Thomson's and Sergeant Cobbin's storerooms.

Sometimes there was several inches above her, sometimes hardly any room at all. But she managed to keep going by humping her bottom and then pushing with her feet and pulling with her hands. It was difficult, but steadily Jane began to hump and push her way slowly down the tube. There was a faint rushing noise in her ears; every now and then this changed its note as the air rushed through the vents into a storeroom. Each time this happened Jane felt for the vents on the left and said through them, softly but clearly, "Hullo—this is Jane Charrington. Is there anyone inside?"

There was never any answer. Jane began to think she'd made a mistake. Of course, she thought, they'd put Captain Thomson and Sergeant Cobbin *farther* away from them so as not to be bothered by them. Or perhaps the ventilation machine sucked air instead of blowing it and so really she was crawling toward the engine room. But it was impossible to turn round, and she'd come much too far to try and go backward. She felt exhausted and frightened. Soon, thought Jane, I shall be too tired to go farther, and then I shall just lie here till I die of thirst.

And then, faint above the rushing air, she heard a strange noise coming from in front. It was a regular purring like a cat or small fan. Very carefully and slowly she humped herself forward.

It was someone snoring. As she came level with the next set of ventilator holes, the steady pulsing note was unmistakable. And Mrs. Deal snored.

"Mrs. Deal, Mrs. Deal," whispered Jane. "Is that you?"

There was no answer.

"Mrs. Deal," said Jane. "*Mrs. Deal,*" she said loudly.

"MRS. DEAL, MRS. DEAL, MRS. DEAL," she shouted, not caring if she woke up every sailor on Peeg.

At last there came a grunting and stirring from the room on the other side of the ventilator holes. Then a deep, familiar voice muttered, "What's that? Who's that?" It was Captain Thomson.

"Captain Thomson," cried Jane. "It me, Jane."

"What?" Captain Thomson's voice was now wide-awake. "Who's there? Where?"

"It's me—Jane. Here," shouted Jane.

She heard Captain Thomson moving rapidly about, muttering loudly. "No one here. I'm going mad. They're breaking me down. Once four is four. Twice four is eight. Three fours . . ."

"Captain Thomson," shouted Jane. "Please. You're not mad. I'm in the ventilation tube. I can't get out. Help."

Luckily, the ventilation tube in Captain Thomson's storeroom was in the open bit of wall and not buried behind boxes of explosive. She heard his voice very close to the vents.

"Is that really you, Jane?"

"Yes," said Jane.

"Goodness me. How wonderful. Come out. Goodness," said Captain Thomson.

"I can't," said Jane. "How can I?"

"Slide it back," said Captain Thomson. "There should be a slideable panel. Wait a minute. The devils have tied me up, but I think I can do it from this side."

There was a lot of grunting and then suddenly a sliding noise just by her ear. Jane stretched out her arm and found it waving in space. The next moment she had struggled out and was leaping about in the darkness.

"Hurrah! Hurrah!" she cried. "Oh, it's wonderful—I thought I'd never find anyone or ever get out."

"You're a good girl, Jane," said Captain Thomson, and

his voice sounded quite shaky. "I'd take you in my arms if the devils hadn't tied my hands."

"Oh, you poor thing," said Jane. "I'll undo them." She felt her way round him and started to work on the rope tightly binding his wrists.

"How'd you get into the ventilation tube?" said Captain Thomson. "Don't tell me that's where the brutes have been keeping you?"

Jane explained, and once again Captain Thomson said he would have hugged her if his hands hadn't still been tied. The knots were very tight, but after half an hour and using her teeth Jane managed to get them undone. Then Captain Thomson did indeed whirl her up and kiss her several times on the top of her head.

"You may have saved our lives," he said.

Jane could feel his beard had grown quite long. "Why are your lights off?" she said. "Mine are left on all the time."

"The silly fools are trying to break me down," said Captain Thomson. "A spot of darkness doesn't bother a chap who's lived underground for thirty-two years, I can tell you.

"Now," went on Captain Thomson in a grim voice, "now we must plan. You wrap yourself in my blanket and lie down opposite the door. I shall hide behind it. Then— we wait."

Trembling with excitement, Jane wrapped herself in the blanket and then sat up against the wall to help him wait. Gradually, however, she sank lower down the wall. Her long hours in the ventilation tube had exhausted her. And it was a great relief to feel she could leave everything to Captain Thomson. In ten minutes she was fast asleep.

At first, excitement kept Captain Thomson wide-awake. One of his worries was that, try as he might, he had completely forgotten every lesson in the unarmed combat leaflets; all the toeholds, armlocks, and various ways of bending, twisting, breaking, and unbalancing an enemy which he had so carefully practiced with Sergeant Cobbin had vanished from his mind. I shall have to rely on surprise, he thought to himself. Let's hope it's one of the smaller sailors. He settled himself for a long night. But he, too, was tired. The strain on him over the past week had been great. During the whole of that afternoon Mr. Tulip had argued with him trying to get him to join Pilut. His head fell onto his chest, and soon his steady snores joined the gentle breathing of Jane in the storeroom.

They were both awakened at seven-thirty by the light being turned on and a sailor walking in with Captain Thomson's breakfast. When he saw Jane he stopped.

"What yer doin' here? This ain't your room."

Jane, who had forgotten where she was, stirred sleepily and said, "Don't be silly—of course it is."

Almost at the same moment Captain Thomson, who had also forgotten, half fell from behind the door, rubbing his eyes.

"What are you doing to me?" he said loudly. "I won't crack. I'm going mad. Where . . ."

At the sound of his voice the sailor whirled round, dropping the breakfast. Immediately Captain Thomson remembered his plans and, recovering just before the sailor, jumped up and grabbed him with his huge hands.

The sailor was neither small nor nearly as old as Captain Thomson. On the other hand, he had been taken by surprise and Captain Thomson was a very big man. They immediately began fighting so fiercely that Jane ran out into the tunnel to see if she could find something to hit the sailor with. But there was nothing to be seen—it stretched empty on either side, still immaculate from Mrs. Deal's last enormous clean.

But by the time she hurried back Captain Thomson was

sitting on the sailor's chest. As she came in, he seized the sailor's revolver from his belt and sprang to the door.

"Get up," he said. "Get up and stand against the wall."

Dazed, the sailor staggered up.

"Tie him up," said Captain Thomson to Jane. "Reef, not Granny. Left over right, right over left."

When she'd finished, Captain Thomson gave her the revolver and told her to shoot if the sailor moved at all.

"Shoot to kill," he said.

Nervously, Jane pointed the heavy gun roughly at the sailor's heart. Captain Thomson went behind him and swiftly added several more knots, pulling the rope tight and then taking the end down and tying it round the sailor's ankles.

When he'd finished, they hurried out and Captain Thomson locked the door behind them.

Outside, he stopped and, looking at Jane, said quietly, "Jane, this is war. We must use our surprise. Counterattack at once, mop up the enemy, then release our friends. Follow me."

They kept well against the rocky wall of the tunnel, stopping every now and again to listen. But they reached the place where the tunnel mouth joined the ramp without seeing anyone, and soon came to the Mess itself. It was as they were creeping along the passage which led to the anteroom that they heard someone whistling.

"The kitchen," whispered Captain Thomson.

Outside the kitchen Captain Thomson placed his fingers on his lips, pointed the revolver in front of him, and boldly pushed the door open.

Standing at the stove with his back toward them stood Bob, the only nice sailor among their guards. He stopped whistling and said without looking round, "You've taken your time, Bill. What kept you?"

166

"Put your hands up," said Captain Thomson. "Don't move. Get a rope from the cupboard, Jane. Hands up, young man. This is war. I shall not hesitate to shoot."

They tied Bob to one of the kitchen chairs, and then Captain Thomson asked how many more sailors were on Peeg.

"Wouldn't you like to know?" Bob said in a tough voice.

"Heat the poker in the stove," said Captain Thomson to Jane. "Push it well in."

"You wouldn't dare," said Bob.

Jane thought this too, but when Captain Thomson pulled the poker out with its handle wrapped in a dish cloth and held it glowing in front of him she became rather nervous.

"Oh, don't burn him, Captain Thomson," she said. "He was always the nicest."

"I'm afraid war is never nice," said Captain Thomson. "It's his life or ours. Go into the anteroom if you don't like the smell of burning flesh. Better still, go somewhere where you won't hear his screams."

But as she was walking away, Bob suddenly said, "All right, all right, I'll talk. You can't escape anyway. No—there's only us two here."

"When are you relieved?" said Captain Thomson.

"Twelve o'clock tomorrow," Bob said.

"Good. We've a whole day," said Captain Thomson. "Do they call?"

"Sometimes," said Bob.

"Very well," said Captain Thomson. "If they ring I shall untie you and you will say that all is well. Is that clear?"

"And if I don't?" said Bob.

Captain Thomson pushed the now cooling poker back into the stove. "You will," he said.

It did not take them long to find the others. They hurried back to the tunnel and, after shouting a bit, traced them by answering shouts.

Jemima burst into tears as Jane rushed in and seized her in her arms.

"Oh, Jane," she sobbed. "I've been so lonely and frightened. Have we been rescued? Oh, that horrid man—he said we'd be blown up in two weeks."

Mrs. Deal was in fighting form. She had spent much of the time polishing and dusting her storeroom with a cloth, and it gleamed spotless when they opened the door.

"And not a minute too soon," she said to Captain Thomson. "I knew you'd get us out—but I had hoped sooner."

"It was Jane here, ma'am," said Captain Thomson. "We owe a great debt to this young lady."

"I shall tell your father and mother," said Mrs. Deal. "Now—where's Mr. Tulip? I'd like to give him the rough side of my tongue. Locking innocent young girls up—the idea! Were you alone?"

Jemima nodded, and at the memory two tears rolled down her cheeks. Mrs. Deal picked her up and hugged her.

"You poor things," she said. "I'll give him a piece of my mind."

Sergeant Cobbin seemed quite unworried by what had happened. He and Captain Thomson shook hands and immediately began to plan what they must do next.

"We've got our war at last, Sergeant," said Captain Thomson.

The long years of training proved their worth. After a quick, but large, breakfast of dried egg, toast, tinned butter, tea, dried milk, and, for a treat, some dried bananas, they all set to work. Sergeant Cobbin, Jane, and Jemima loaded the Peeg Special with petrol. This meant quite a long walk carrying heavy cans round the back of Mount Peeg so that there would be less chance of their being seen from *Tulip*. Captain Thomson got out his maps and tried to work out where they were and where they could fly to. Mrs. Deal took the first watch at the top of the Blowup Room stairs, where their secret entrance opened onto the cliff. She was to give warning if anyone came from the submarine.

All day they worked, taking it in turns to watch from the clifftop. The machinery to blow up the island had to be carefully checked. Warm clothes were got out of the store and tried on. "We start at first light," Captain Thomson had said. Maps, torches, binoculars, and the engine room compass—which had been replaced while they were locked up—were all loaded into the Peeg Special's tiny cabin. Sergeant Cobbin gave them each a machine gun, a revolver, and fifty rounds of ammunition. The telephone rang twice, but each time Captain Thomson seized the poker and made Bob tell them everything was all right.

By evening it was all completed. They went to bed early after a large supper.

"An army marches on its stomach," said Captain Thomson. "Tomorrow the outcome of the battle will be decided."

They were up early. Jane and Jemima were so excited they woke at four o'clock and couldn't get to sleep again. But, in any case, Mrs. Deal came into their room at five o'clock while they were busy talking and told them to get up quickly.

"The Captain wants to start at seven sharp," she said.

"Gosh, how *exciting* it is," said Jane.

"It is extremely dangerous," said Mrs. Deal in a rather disapproving voice. But when she had helped them both dress, in thick woolly underpants, khaki trousers, and thick quilted wind jackets, she said, "Well, yes—there is certainly an element of excitement. As you know, the Navy has always been my favorite among the services owing to my husband, followed closely, now, by the Army. But I've always had a soft spot for the Air Force. What do you think of these?"

She put her hand into the large pocket of her apron, which she was wearing over the same flying uniform that Jane and Jemima had on, and pulled out a large pair of goggles. She put them on and went over to the looking glass.

"Quite becoming," said Mrs. Deal. "It wouldn't surprise me if they became the vogue." She turned her head sideways and patted her bun. Then she took two more pairs of goggles from her pocket and gave one each to the two girls. "We're all to have them. In case the windows break in the Peeg Special."

Captain Thomson's plan, as usual, was simple but brilliant. The blowup mechanism was to be set for a waiting period of twenty minutes. He was then going to ring up the submarine and tell them Peeg would blow up in twenty minutes and they would just have time to rescue the two sailors and escape themselves. Meanwhile the Peeg party would escape in the plane. The plan was possible because the blowup machinery was of a very special sort. Once started, it could not be stopped, not even if the Blowup Room itself was completely destroyed, because when the Blowup Room switch was pressed, a timing mechanism was started in every single storeroom. To stop the island blowing up then, all those timing machines would have to be found and destroyed, and they had all been hidden in the rock of each storeroom.

"When they come and get you," Captain Thomson said, after explaining all this to Bob, "you pass it on. Right?"

"Right," said Bob, who had become quite docile.

Unfortunately, there were still some adjustments to be made to the blowup machinery, and at eight-thirty Captain Thomson and Sergeant Cobbin were still working feverishly at them. Jane and Jemima were both keeping watch at the top of the Blowup Room stairs.

Luckily, it was neither raining nor snowing, but dark clouds poured across the sky hardly a hundred feet above the turbulent sea. They could see several icebergs rising out of the waves, some quite large, some no more than chunks, pitching and tossing like small boats.

Jane was looking lazily out, passing the binoculars back and forth over the just visible top of the submarine, when she noticed to her surprise that it seemed to be rising higher and higher out of the water. When it was rough the *Tulip* often went completely underwater to pull Peeg, only coming up when it was necessary to send a boat ashore. This happened now. Before their horrified eyes, a boat containing three tiny figures was lowered from the submarine and in a moment was roaring toward the island. Not, however, before Jane had recognized one of the men through her glasses.

"It's Mr. Tulip," she said to Jemima, as they raced down the Blowup Room stairs.

Captain Thomson was brisk and calm. "Plan C, Sergeant," he said. "Mrs. Deal, girls—hide a hundred yards down the tunnel. If we are captured, come and release us. Sergeant—you go inside that cupboard. I shall conceal myself in the anteroom. They will go first to the kitchen because that is where the guards have been sitting.

171

I shall come quietly to the door and step smartly in. The moment you hear my voice, Sergeant, step from the cupboard to complete the pincer movement."

It all went as Captain Thomson had planned. Crouching in the tunnel, clutching their guns nervously to their chests, Jane, Jemima, and Mrs. Deal could just pick out the murmur of voices, among them the high, gay notes of Mr. Tulip. Then after a pause they heard Captain Thomson's loud giving-orders voice. About five minutes later Sergeant Cobbin called down the tunnel.

"Mrs. Deal? You can all come back now. Job's done."

Two new sailors and Mr. Tulip were standing against the wall with their hands up. Captain Thomson, a revolver pointing at them, looked at his watch.

"Time to get cracking," he said. "Tie up those two sailors, Sergeant; then, Jane, Jemima, you go and get the Peeg Special out."

"What about me, my dear?" said Mr. Tulip. "What dreadful fate have you in store for me?"

"You're coming with us, Tulip," said Captain Thomson shortly. "Sergeant—tie his hands behind his back. Mrs. Deal—do you feel strong enough to guard him?"

"Oh, dear," said Mrs. Deal. "Using my—that is, might I have to fire my gun?"

"I hope not," said Captain Thomson. "But you know how to. Only shoot him in the legs."

"Oh, dear," said Mrs. Deal. "I *think* I could. I'll try."

"Plucky girl," said Captain Thomson. "March him to the top of the Blowup stairs and you can watch the submarine at the same time. I shall adjust the timing mechanism, set it, and then—off we go!"

Mrs. Deal pointed her gun at Mr. Tulip's knees. "Quick march, Mr. Tulip," she said firmly. "To the anteroom. Walk in front of me."

Jemima, Jane, and Sergeant Cobbin all hurried up onto the cliff and ran up to the cave where the Peeg Special had been concealed. It was very heavy, but fortunately the ground sloped downhill and, once they had pulled the wooden blocks away from in front of the wheels, it rolled downhill itself with Sergeant Cobbin sitting in the pilot's seat to put the brakes on.

They had just turned it round and were arranging things inside the tiny cabin when suddenly, so loud it made them all jump, there came the sound of furious shooting from farther back along the clifftop. Sergeant Cobbin seized his gun and jumped from the plane.

"Glory me," they heard him say. "Mrs. Deal's gorn off her rocker."

The old-fashioned machine guns were short little guns which could fire thirty bullets one after another. They had lots of knobs and clips and used to rattle a lot. They often went wrong and in nervous hands would suddenly start firing for no reason at all and were almost impossible to stop.

This was what had happened to Mrs. Deal. Looking across to the rocks and bushes which concealed the Blowup Room entrance, they saw Mr. Tulip come rushing out, closely followed by Mrs. Deal. Mrs. Deal's gun was firing continuously, but instead of throwing it away, she was swinging it wildly about, so that bullets whirled past Mr. Tulip and even tore into the ground at her own feet. The firing stopped. Mr. Tulip turned and bolted back into the bushes around the Blowup stairs door.

Mrs. Deal continued running toward the plane.

But worse was to follow. The sound of the gun had alerted the submarine. As they watched, the bridge rose up on its top. They could see men running about under the glass dome, and then panels opened along the side of the submarine and three large boats crammed with sailors slid out.

"Go and get the Captain," Sergeant Cobbin shouted to Jane. "Jemima, you help me get this stuff stowed. I'll start her engines. Hurry."

Jane shouted, "Help Jemima and Sergeant Cobbin get everything arranged," to Mrs. Deal as she passed. But Mrs. Deal, face set, her bun beginning to unravel, ran on toward the plane without answering.

When Jane reached the anteroom Mr. Tulip, shaking and trembling, was on his knees before Captain Thomson. "Save me! Save me!" he was crying. "She's gone mad. She tried to kill me. Don't leave me. I won't do anything."

When Jane rushed in he gave a loud scream and tried to crawl behind Captain Thomson's legs, only stopping when he saw it was Jane.

"Oh, thank goodness, darling," he said. "I thought you were that lunatic. What's she doing? Reloading?"

"Boats are coming from the submarine," panted Jane. "Sergeant Cobbin's starting the engines."

"Right," said Captain Thomson. "I'm coming at once. Get back to the plane and help. Tulip—get up. You'll stay by me."

When Jane arrived back at the Peeg Special its engine was roaring and it was straining against the large rocks which had been put in front of its wheels. Looking across to the submarine, Jane saw that the boats were well on their way to the island.

"Where's the Captain?" shouted Sergeant Cobbin above the roar of the engine.

"He's coming," shouted Jane.

But there was no sign of Captain Thomson. The boats bounced and tossed on the waves, surging forward with their powerful engines. Sergeant Cobbin unslung his gun from his shoulder.

"Mrs. Deal," he called. "Take Jemima's gun and come and help me head them off. Girls—you stay here."

"I'm not touching one of those weapons again as long as I live," shouted Mrs. Deal, who had already climbed into the Peeg Special.

Sergeant Cobbin hesitated, then said, "Right—Jane and Jemima, give me your guns and stay here."

The two girls stood and watched him run to the cliff-top. The plane roared and shuddered behind them. They couldn't hear Sergeant Cobbin's gun, but the boats began to swerve and dodge. He threw away one gun and picked up another. Still the boats drew nearer, and suddenly Jane heard a noise like a whip cracking above her head. The sailors were firing back.

And then at last Captain Thomson appeared from the Blowup Room. He was staggering under two immense loads; under one arm, kicking and struggling, was Mr. Tulip; under the other he held a huge sack.

He and Sergeant Cobbin reached the plane at the same time.

"Help me get this man in," Captain Thomson shouted.

"I won't. I won't," shouted Mr. Tulip, struggling violently. "Won't, won't, won't."

But Sergeant Cobbin seized his shoulders and Captain Thomson his legs and they threw him into the cabin. Captain Thomson bent down and picked up his sack.

"What's that?" shouted Sergeant Cobbin.

"A few rocks," shouted Captain Thomson. "My geological specimens."

"We're not taking those," shouted Sergeant Cobbin. "We'll be lucky if we get off as it is."

"It's thirty-two years' work," shouted Captain Thomson.

"I'm not trying to take off with that," Sergeant Cobbin shouted back.

They stood glaring at each other, Captain Thomson clutching his sack as though it were a large baby. But at that moment they heard the sound of guns above the roar of the engine. The sailors had climbed the cliff and were kneeling along its top, firing at them.

"Get in the plane," yelled Captain Thomson, dropping his sack of geological specimens. "Girls—this is fire and movement." He wrenched his gun off his shoulders and sent a shower of bullets along the clifftop. The sailors ducked down.

Sergeant Cobbin sprang into the plane, and a moment later the engine died to a loud mutter.

"Jane, Jemima," Sergeant Cobbin shouted from his cockpit. "Pull away the stones."

The two girls did so and then, terrified now by the sailors' bullets, which despite Captain Thomson's firing were still hitting the ground all round them, rushed to the plane. Mrs. Deal pulled them in. Captain Thomson fired a last burst of bullets, bent down, flung his sack of rocks into the cabin on top of Mr. Tulip, and pulled himself in, slamming the door behind him. The engine rose to a roar, and very slowly they began to bump along the grass.

Through the tiny window Jane saw the sailors spring up from along the edge of the little cliff and start to run after the plane. The Peeg Special trundled a bit faster, but still firmly on the ground. Faster—the sailors were left behind but now knelt and fired. Faster—the engine roaring, the cabin shaking, but still they were on the ground. Jane and Jemima, noses pressed to the windows, could see the grass whizzing by, feel the bumps as they raced over the stones and holes. They must be getting near the end of the cliff. Oh, why, Jane thought, had Captain Thomson thrown all the rocks in? Faster.

Suddenly Sergeant Cobbin looked round and yelled into the cabin, "I can't do it. I can't get her off. We're too heavy."

It was too late to do anything. With engine roaring, the Peeg Special reached the end of the cliff and roared straight over the edge. There was a sudden sinking in their stomachs as it fell toward the sea. And then, as the waves actually broke over the wheels, it stopped falling. They raced along just above the white crests and at last, slowly, slowly, began to rise into the air. Higher and higher they rose, turning all the time, until four minutes later Sergeant Cobbin was able to fly back quite high above the island on course for Australia.

Captain Thomson looked at his watch. "We've got ten minutes till she blows up," he shouted. "Keep her on full throttle, Sergeant. We don't want to be hoist with our own petard."

Looking down on Peeg, Jane and Jemima could just make out the sailors rushing out from the Mess and running across the cliff and the beach to their boats. The submarine already looked quite small.

"They may just make it," cried Captain Thomson above the roar of the engine. "But they've got to cast off and then dive deep. Very deep and very fast. I doubt they'll do it."

Jane could see where the school had been before the hurricane had blown it away. Its foundations were clearly outlined on the turf. She could see Captain Thomson's garden. She could see the top of Mount Peeg where Sergeant Cobbin had sunbathed. She could see the foam at the back of the island where the gallant engines still

forced the island on. She realized that she had grown very fond of Peeg and hardly wanted to see it blown up.

She looked at Captain Thomson. His red face was set and expressionless. Every now and then he looked at his watch. He held the binoculars to his eyes and stared back at Peeg as it disappeared behind them.

Jemima looked back too, sharing one of the little windows with Jane now, because Mrs. Deal and Mr. Tulip had revived sufficiently to crouch next to each other, and Captain Thomson had the third. The island grew smaller and smaller. First the submarine seemed to merge with it, then the cliff became hard to distinguish. Below them the sea was gray and wrinkled, with occasional icebergs like toys on the crumpled blanket of a giant's bed. It became difficult to make out the mountain. The whole of Peeg looked like a mound in the distance. Captain Thomson looked at his watch. The mound became a loaf.

"She's going in thirty seconds," Captain Thomson shouted to Sergeant Cobbin. Sergeant Cobbin switched the automatic steering on and turned to look back through his cockpit window.

The loaf became a fist. "Now!" cried Captain Thomson.

But still Peeg sat there, still distinguishable in the gray distance. For at least a minute they watched it. Jane thought, It won't go up. They've made a mistake.

And then, very slowly, the island began to swell. It grew twice, three times its normal size, until silently, almost gently it opened up in the middle and a vast white ball, too bright to look at, grew out of the opening. Then the white ball began to shoot upward, creating as it went a great shaft of black smoke like the trunk of a thick tree in which flames and sudden balls of fire appeared and vanished.

They heard the first rumble of the explosion above the

engine, and then the plane was suddenly seized by a blast of air and whirled violently sideways. Jane and Jemima were flung together across the cabin, and the plane fell toward the sea.

For five minutes they were tossed and buffeted by the winds from the explosion. Sergeant Cobbin wrestled with the controls. They caught glimpses of the island through the windows, the fireball splitting up and expanding, the black cloud rising higher and higher. The rumbling grew fainter.

Gradually the air became calmer, the plane flew level. Sergeant Cobbin throttled the engine back to save petrol and its roar sank to a steady drone.

Jane and Jemima looked out of the little window and back over the sea. The fire and flashing of the explosion had gone. A vast, perfect mushroom cloud had formed in the sky such as they had seen in pictures of atomic bombs and was now beginning to drift northward, its shape slowly distorting in the winds. Of the Island of Peeg there was no sign.

10

HOME AGAIN

THERE IS NOT a great deal more to tell.

The journey to Australia was long and uncomfortable. Jane sat on Mrs. Deal's lap and Jemima on Captain Thomson's. Mr. Tulip sat in a little space on the floor, surrounded by food, tins of petrol, and pressed into by Captain Thomson's sack of rocks.

It was extremely cold at first. Luckily their clothes were very warm, but Mr. Tulip soon began to shiver and shake in his thin silk uniform.

"You should wear more sensible clothes," said Captain Thomson, who had secretly always rather disapproved of the white uniform.

"My dear, if I'd known you were planning this little trip I'd have put on something cosier," said Mr. Tulip irritably, his teeth chattering.

After a while, Captain Thomson put his rock specimens all round the cabin and gave Mr. Tulip the sack to wrap round his shoulders.

On and on droned the Peeg Special. It began to grow dark. Sergeant Cobbin had fitted a tube from the reserve fuel tank into the cabin so that he could pour petrol down it from the cans. They had enough fuel to take them two thousand miles, but with all the extra weight Sergeant Cobbin thought it would be touch and go.

They had supper and then sat uneasily dozing, listening to the engine and trying to keep warm. At two o'clock in the morning Sergeant Cobbin clambered stiffly back from his cockpit and asked Captain Thomson to take over. Captain Thomson was a little worried, although he had been taught what to do. But nothing happened, and at four o'clock Sergeant Cobbin took over again.

At ten o'clock that morning, just twenty-four and a half hours after they had left Peeg, the west coast of Australia rose up over the horizon. Half an hour later, with one can of petrol left, they bumped to a stop in a small field outside the little town of Nornabys.

After a bath, a sleep, and a large lunch, they were driven north to Perth and then flown for questioning to Canberra. Here, the first thing they insisted on doing was sending telegrams to tell everyone they were alive. Mrs. Deal sent one to her brother Frank in Peeblesshire. Jane and Jemima sent one to their parents. Captain Thomson and Sergeant Cobbin said sadly that they didn't suppose anyone would remember them, but in the end they sent one to the War Office.

The police and Australian Secret Service seemed to believe nothing. But everyone in Canberra was very excited by the explosion of Peeg, which the scientists had thought was a Chinese atom bomb. Captain Thomson was able to point out on the map more or less where it had happened, and this agreed with the scientists' calculations. Secret documents Captain Thomson had brought from Peeg also impressed them.

But it was Mr. Tulip they were most interested in and

who finally made them take everything else seriously. The Pilut organization had already been in touch with the Australian government and they had been very worried. At first they didn't believe Mr. Tulip *was* Mr. Tulip, until photographs and other details, despite Mr. Tulip's strenuous denials, proved who he was. Then their whole attitude changed at once.

"Do you mean he really did the things he said he did?" Jane asked the officer who was questioning them.

"He is a dangerous international criminal," said the officer. "Precisely what he's been up to it's difficult to say. But he is wanted in several countries and, whether or not the rest of your extraordinary story is true, you have done a great service in catching him."

Mr. Tulip was taken away from them that same evening. He looked so forlorn, and at the same time brave, in his crumpled uniform, that Jane and Jemima ran after him to the door.

"Good-bye, Mr. Tulip," said Jemima.

"Come and see us when they let you out of prison," said Jane.

Mr. Tulip looked pleased and, bending down, kissed them each gently on the cheek. "Thank you, darlings," he whispered. "But don't worry. They won't keep me long. I promise you, darlings, I'll see you before the year is out."

When he'd gone, Mrs. Deal said, "I've a feeling we'll see that rogue again. He's a bad penny—whatever his charm."

Their story sounded so fantastic (especially as a telegram to London had discovered that no one there had even heard of "Operation Peeg") and at the same time was so important, since it was not only about the Pilut plan to nearly destroy Australia, but about British wartime secrets as well, that it was decided to fly them to London. Their presence had been kept secret and they were flown out two nights later in a large airliner, in which, to Mrs. Deal's excitement, they traveled first class. Before they left they were allowed to send telegrams telling their relations when they would arrive.

Although the Australians were now very polite, Jane could see that they were still suspicious. Two policemen went with them, though they sat discreetly behind them all the way.

"They think we're part of the Pilut organization," said Captain Thomson angrily. "I bet Tulip's been spinning some tale."

A great many times during their questioning he'd said sternly to the Australians, "We are serving members of His Majesty's Armed Forces."

"Her Majesty's," said Jane.

"Her Majesty's then," said Captain Thomson, impatiently swinging his goggles.

The first thing that happened at London Airport was Mr. and Mrs. Garing. Jemima rushed into their arms, bursting into tears, and Mr. and Mrs. Garing were both crying too.

"Darling, darling," sobbed Mr. Garing.

But there was no sign of Jane's mother and father, and though she asked all the policemen and airport people they said there had been no message.

"They must be in America still," said Mrs. Deal, holding Jane in her arms. "You'll see them soon."

"Yes, I will, won't I?" said Jane, trying not to cry. And then she suddenly burst into tears, and, clinging to Mrs. Deal, sobbed, "I will see them soon. I will."

There was a telegram for Mrs. Deal which said: "Thank you for telegram. Had no idea you were meant to be dead. Frank."

"Well, I suppose I must be glad he was spared the agony of uncertainty," said Mrs. Deal, somewhat put out.

Jemima was allowed to drive from the airport with her mother and father, though they had to drive between the large black car in which the others drove and a police car following.

"VIP treatment," said Mrs. Deal, settling back into the large comfortable seat. "I feel quite the little pop star."

"Pop stars aren't followed by police," said Jane. "We're more like famous criminals."

"Well, as long as we're famous," said Mrs. Deal dreamily.

All the way Captain Thomson and Sergeant Cobbin were amazed at the changes, especially as they got deeper and deeper into London. "Do you remember poor old London when we last saw her, Sergeant?" Captain Thomson said.

"The blitz?" said Sergeant Cobbin. "She took a proper beating right enough."

"Brave boys of Biggin Hill," said Captain Thomson. "Look—they've dug a hole under Hyde Park Corner."

At Whitehall, where Jemima's parents had to stay behind in a waiting room, they were hurried through long corridors and eventually shown into a large room overlooking St. James's Park. Captain Thomson paced nervously up and down.

"Brings it back, eh?" said Sergeant Cobbin. Captain Thomson nodded. Mrs. Deal still had a dreamy smile on her face and was moving very slowly and gracefully. Somewhat to his embarrassment, she had given her arm to the young man who had led them to the room.

"I feel like a queen," she'd whispered to Jane and Jemima.

They hadn't waited long when the door opened and a tall, gray-haired man in uniform, with a large red face, walked heavily in and stopped, looking at them all.

"Good morning," he said. "I'm General Herkenshaw. How do you do?" He looked at them rather grimly again, and then suddenly leaned forward, staring at Captain Thomson. He took two slow steps, still staring, and then suddenly bellowed, "It's Tony Thomson! Tony! My dear fellow—where have you been all these years?"

Captain Thomson was also advancing, his face red and jolly. "Bill!" he cried. "Bill a General. I'd never have believed it. Wonderful to see you, old man."

They shook hands and almost embraced. Then General Herkenshaw turned to Sergeant Cobbin and said, "No—don't tell me. Wait a moment. It's on the tip of my tongue—*Cobbin*. That's it—it's Cobbin, isn't it?"

"Sir!" cried Sergeant Cobbin, pink in the face and standing stiffly to attention.

"Sergeant Cobbin of D Squadron," said the General.

"Sir!" yelled Sergeant Cobbin, standing even more stiffly.

"At ease, Sergeant, at ease," said the General kindly. "Now, Tony—introduce me."

"This is Mrs. Deal," said Captain Thomson. "This is Miss Jemima Garing; this is Miss Jane Charrington."

"Not the ex-Earl's daughter, not Chris Charrington?" cried General Herkenshaw, again amazed.

"Yes," said Jane.

"By all that's wonderful," said the General. "I know your father well, young lady. He's due back from America soon with your dear mother. It's all very hush-hush, of course—as usual. But within a week. But what is all this, Tony? I was told you were possible defecting Pilut agents. Perhaps the leaders."

"It's a long story, Bill," said Captain Thomson.

"And you must tell it," said the General. "But you must be tired. You, madam—have you had a bath?"

"A bath would certainly be gratefully appreciated," said Mrs. Deal graciously.

"Where are these good people staying?" the General said over his shoulder to the Lieutenant who had accompanied him.

"Well, sir," said the Lieutenant, "the Minister said they were to be kept in custody."

"Nonsense, nonsense," cried General Herkenshaw. "These are friends of mine. Tony and I went to Aldershot together—and then to India, eh, Tony? No—get Sergeant Cobbin, Mrs. Deal, Miss Garing, and Miss Charrington rooms in the Ritz. Tony, you'd better come along with me."

"Jemima's mother and father are here, Bill," Captain Thomson said.

"Then she must stay with them," said General Herkenshaw, "and, no doubt, until her mother and father get back, young Jane would like to stay with them too."

So began their two days of questioning. But it was much easier and nicer than in Australia. Captain Thomson told General Herkenshaw almost everything over their lunch, and for the rest of the time they just had to be there in case there were more questions.

It was soon discovered that the train carrying the workers who had made Operation Peeg back to England had been totally destroyed by a bomb. This the two soldiers knew already. But it was then discovered that the building in which the Operation would have been planned, and where all its records would have been kept, had also been totally destroyed. So secret had Operation Peeg been that the only other living person who knew about it had been

Winston Churchill, and they supposed, in the turmoil of war, he had forgotten about it.

"If we'd known about Operation Peeg," said General Herkenshaw, "of course we'd have made a search. We'd have thought twice about the falling-to-bits theory the scientists suggested."

It was also found out that the Island of Peeg had been seen at least five times during their journey south. Two ships had seen it and three aeroplanes. But when anyone tried to see the new island again it had of course moved on and no one could find it.

Then, on the second day, a copy of a short letter was found in Winston Churchill's private papers. It said that, in view of the progress of the war, Operation Peeg was no longer necessary and should be discontinued immediately. The letter was dated the very day on which the whole building to do with Operation Peeg was destroyed by a flying bomb.

"It must have been delivered and then immediately destroyed in the explosion," said General Herkenshaw, "before anything could be done. That explains why Winston did nothing more. He imagined his orders had been carried out. I thought the old boy wouldn't have forgotten something like this, which must have been very dear to his heart."

But Captain Thomson and Sergeant Cobbin were very depressed by the discovery of Winston Churchill's letter. They felt it meant they had been wasting their time. General Herkenshaw soon cheered them up.

"On the contrary," he said. "Yours is the spirit which won us the war. It's what I'd have expected of you both, and I hope I'd have had the guts to do the same. What is more, you have caught—you five have caught—a very dangerous criminal we have been after for some years.

The man Tulip. I shall see you are rewarded for both actions."

Captain Thomson was promoted to full Colonel, and Sergeant Cobbin, at his own request not made an officer, to Regimental Sergeant-Major. Captain Thomson was awarded the Distinguished Service Cross and Sergeant Cobbin the Distinguished Conduct Medal. Their pay was also given them for the whole thirty-two years they had been on the island. In addition to this, there was a reward of fifty thousand pounds for the capture of Mr. Tulip, which they all shared.

"It's no more than you deserve," said General Herkenshaw. "And I'm glad that this little bonus, plus gratuity, demob pay, back pay, and no doubt some journalist and TV fees will make you, Tony, and you, Sergeant-Major Cobbin, comparatively wealthy men."

The news was then given to the public, and for three days they were interviewed, photographed, and appeared on TV. Only Mrs. Deal seemed to enjoy it.

Mr. and Mrs. Garing, who had been very kind to Jane, took Jemima away home soon after the questioning was over. They said that Miss Boyle had started a new school on an island called Isle Ornsay off Skye, but that Jemima wasn't going to it. They asked Jane to come and stay, but she said she'd wait in London till her mother and father came back. And, two days later, they did.

When Jane met her father and mother at the airport she was so pleased and exited she forgot everything else. Mr. Charrington whirled her high into the air and kissed her from the top of her head to the tips of her toes. Mrs. Charrington held her close and said, "My darling, my little darling."

Soon it was all explained. Mr. Charrington was a very

distinguished space scientist. The government had suddenly sent him on an extremely urgent and secret space mission to America. So secret and urgent was the mission, in fact, that the arrangements for sending him letters hadn't worked. No one knew where he was—except those too busy and secret and important to bother with forwarding letters. As a result, he and Mrs. Charrington had never got Miss Boyle's telegram and letter, nor Jane's telegram, and as they hadn't often read the English papers, they hadn't any idea anything was wrong at all.

"Except we did think you were writing rather few letters," said Mr. Charrington. "But then you always do that, my sweet."

It all came out in General Herkenshaw's flat, where they had driven from the airport. Mr. Charrington was immediately furious and made several angry telephone calls. Mrs. Charrington held her daughter in her arms again. "How could you bear it, darling?" she said.

"Well, Mrs. Deal would say it's a mercy you were spared the agony of uncertainty," said Jane. "But I'd have liked you not to have been spared *all* of it. You could have had a twinge, and then you'd have been even more pleased to see me."

"We *couldn't* be more pleased," said Mrs. Charrington, hugging her again.

"It won't happen again," said Mr. Charrington.

Captain Thomson and Sergeant Cobbin (or rather Colonel and R.S.M) were in General Herkenshaw's flat too. And soon Mr. and Mrs. Charrington were listening enthralled and amazed to their daughter's adventures. When the tale was ended, Mr. Charrington walked over to the two soldiers and shook their hands.

"Colonel, R.S.M," he said, "you've brought our daughter through safely. I'm deeply grateful."

"Your daughter brought us through safely," said Colonel Thomson. "If it wasn't for her we'd still be locked in the storerooms inside Peeg. She's a fine girl."

"If it weren't for her I'd be at the bottom of the sea," said R.S.M. Cobbin.

Jane blushed modestly and then said quickly, "Can they come and stay at Aldeburgh with us, Daddy?"

"They're more than welcome," said Mr. Charrington. "I hope we'll see a great deal of them before we go. But that's a piece of news I haven't had time to tell you. We're off to Cape Kennedy next week for two years. You, Mummy, Mrs. Deal, and me."

"Oh! But they must come too," cried Jane, suddenly realizing she couldn't bear not to see the two soldiers again.

"Don't you worry, Miss Jane," said R.S.M Cobbin. "We'll all meet again."

They spent one more day in London, and then it was time to go down to Aldeburgh.

The two soldiers came to Liverpool Street to say good-bye. As they all stood on the platform Jane felt very sad. Even if they did just meet once or twice, she felt they wouldn't meet often. The two soldiers were upset too. When the whistle blew and R.S.M Cobbin picked her up his face was quite red and his voice was hoarse.

"Now off you go, Miss Jane," he whispered. "We'll see you very soon."

She thought she saw tears in Colonel Thomson's eyes as well.

"There's a good girl," was all he could say as he held her in his big arms. "There's a good girl."

The train was moving. They were all in a first-class carriage. Jane suddenly burst into tears.

"We must see them again," she sobbed. "For a nice long time. Always."

"We will, darling," said Mrs. Charrington gently.

"We'll have them out to Cape Kennedy for a long holiday."

"Promise?" said Jane.

"Promise," said Mrs. Charrington, and at once Jane felt better.

"Now you come in," said Mr. Charrington. "Don't want your head knocked off. Come and sit by me, my sweet."

But Jane kept her head out a little longer and went on waving and waving until the two old soldiers grew smaller and smaller and eventually, as the train went round a corner, disappeared altogether.